BLACKMAILED
BY THE
GREEK'S VOWS

BLACKMAILED BY THE GREEK'S VOWS

TARA PAMMI

MILLS & BOON

First published in Great Britain 2018
by Mills & Boon, an imprint of HarperCollins*Publishers*
1 London Bridge Street, London, SE1 9GF

Large Print edition 2018

© 2018 Tara Pammi

ISBN: 978-0-263-07425-3

For all the readers
who asked for Valentina's story.

CHAPTER ONE

SHE WAS DRESSED like a...a hooker.

No...not exactly a hooker.

No hooker he knew possessed the class, the style and the innate grace that imbued every one of his wife's movements.

More of a high-class escort.

It took Kairos Constantinou a few seconds to clear the red haze that descended in front of his eyes.

Dios...of all the stunts he had expected his impulsive, fiery wife to pull, it hadn't been this.

When his PI had informed him that he'd located Valentina and that she'd be aboard Kairos's own yacht for the party tonight, he hadn't been surprised.

Valentina had always been the life of the party scene in Milan.

Lively. Sensual. Like a beautiful butterfly that flits from flower to flower. The minute her brother Leandro had pointed her out to Kairos, standing amidst a gaggle of men, Kairos had decided he wanted her.

Three minutes into Leandro introducing them, he'd known she was going to be his wife.

She had been the best possible incentive Leandro could have offered to reel Kairos into the alliance. Kairos would gain entry into the rarefied old-world alliances that her family the Conti dynasty, swam in, and she would get a rich husband.

Not once had he questioned why Leandro had thought he needed to set up his beautiful sister like that.

All Kairos had wanted was the prize that was Valentina Conti.

Except, a week into his marriage, he had realized his wife was anything but a trophy.

She was emotionally fiery, intensely vulnerable and impulsive as hell.

The best example of which was her deserting him nine months ago without so much as a word.

And to find her here among this crowd now.

With instincts he'd honed among the street gangs of Athens, he noted three Russian investors who operated businesses barely this side of legal—the men his friend Max intended to wine and dine—another man who was a model and a friend of Valentina's, and five women to entertain them, not counting Valentina.

Women of the oldest profession known to man. Not streetwalkers, like some of his earliest friends, but undoubtedly from an escort service.

And the most provocatively dressed among them was Valentina in a flimsy gold dress.

The slinky material pooled at her chest to create a low neckline that left her shoulders and her toned arms bare. It pushed up those small breasts that he had touched and kissed and sucked while she writhed under him, like a lover's hands.

So much golden, soft, silky skin… His jaw tightened like a vise as three other men salivated over her.

But it was the smiles she bestowed on the men as she charmed them, those arms flying about in that way of hers while she narrated some escapade in her accented English, full of fire, the way she put a hand on Max's arm and thanked him when he refilled her drink…that was what caused the ice to stiffen his spine.

The wall of detachment that had always been his armor against anything was his only defense.

No, this was only want. Physical want…nothing more.

He still wanted her, desperately, because she was Valentina and even with her explosive tempers and childish tantrums, she had still snuck under his skin.

He needed her as his wife for a few months. And in those few months, he'd work her out of his blood. Out of his life.

If Valentina Conti Constantinou had indulged in some fantasy delusion that her husband Kairos had arrived on the yacht to achieve some sort of romantic reunion between them, he burned the notion to ashes within the first few minutes.

It had been disturbing enough to find that not only had her photographer friend Nikolai, at whose persuasion she had come to the party, manipulated her into wearing the tackiest outfit, but that she was surrounded by women from an escort service *and* men expected to be *entertained* by them.

She'd squared her shoulders, made Nikolai *claim* her for the evening, and had begun to charm the Russians. The one thing she knew how to do. She might have been living on nothing for months but she had class. Years of practice at playing the perfect socialite—well-versed in fashion and politics.

Until Kairos had walked in.

Barely sipping her G&T, she nodded at something Nikolai whispered in her ear, keeping her effusive smile firmly in place. Her throat was raw with the falsely pitched laughs, and her chest hurt at having to play the unruffled socialite the way she had all her life.

Every inch of her rebelled against the calm she had assumed from the moment Kairos had stepped onto the deck. Every cell in her roared to swat away the woman who was even now cozying up to him, far too pleased with herself.

She wanted to announce to the rest of them that he was hers.

But he had never belonged to her.

Her grip shook, clinking the ice in her tumbler. Tina put her glass down, fighting for control.

Men scrambled around Max for an introduction to Kairos, and the women—hair fluffed, breasts pushed up to spill out of already plunging necklines—it was as if the rough, rugged masculinity of him was an inviting caress to every woman.

Dios mio, the strength of his sheer masculine

appeal hit her like a punch now, shaking her up, turning her inside out.

His white shirt stretched tight across his broad shoulders, enhancing his raw, rugged appeal. His expansive chest tapered down to a narrow waist, over leaner hips and then he was all legs. Hard, muscular thighs followed by those runner's calves that had once driven her crazy.

His hair was cut into that short style he preferred. Her fingers twitched, remembering the rough sensation of it, and she fisted them at her side. His gaze flicked down to her hands and then back up her body, slowly, possessively.

Those silvery eyes lingered on the long stretch of her legs, her thighs, noted the short hem of the dress, up to her waist, lingered again over her breasts, moved up her neck and then settled again on her face.

If he had run those hands over her body with that rough urgency that he'd always mastered before he lost control, she couldn't have felt more owned. With one look, he plunged her into that state of mindless longing, that state of anticipation he had become used to expecting from her.

Shivering inside her skin, forgetting all the misery he had inflicted on her, Tina lifted her chin in defiance.

He had never liked her to dress provocatively. Had never liked her easy attitude with other men, that almost flirty style of talking that was her nature. They had had more than one row on the subject of her dresses, her hair, her shoes, her style, her attitude and even her body.

One of the blondes she had genuinely liked earlier—Stella of the big boobs and even bigger hips—tapped his arm. A smile curving his thin lips, he sliced his gaze away in clear, decisive dismissal.

Tears scratched up Tina's throat and she hurriedly looked away before someone could see her mortification.

Nine months ago, she'd have slapped the woman's face—she cringed at the memory of doing that to her sister-in-law Sophia, having been induced into a jealous, insecure rage. She'd have screamed and made a spectacle of herself, she'd have let her temper get the better of her and proved to everyone and Kairos how crazy she was about him.

Nine months ago, she'd have let the hot emotions spiraling through her dictate her every word, every move.

Nine months ago, she'd been under the stupid delusion that Kairos had married her because he wanted her, because he felt something for her, even if he didn't put it in words.

But no, he had married her as part of an alliance with her brother Leandro. Even after learning that bitter truth, she could have given her marriage a try.

But Kairos didn't possess a heart. Didn't know what to do with one given into his keeping.

She had humiliated herself, she had prostrated her every thought, every feeling at his feet. And it hadn't been enough.

She hadn't been enough.

"So you're truly over with him...that glowering husband of yours."

"Si," Tina said automatically. And then wished she hadn't.

When the party began winding down, she had slipped below deck with the excuse of visiting the ladies' room and hidden herself away in the lovely gray-and-blue bedroom, her nerves frayed to the hilt at the constant awareness of Kairos.

It was tiring to play the stoic, unaffected party girl. To stuff away all the longing and hurt and anger into a corner of her heart.

But Nikolai had followed her downstairs.

Although over the last couple of months she'd realized that Nikolai was harmless, he was drunk now. Her brother Luca had taught her long ago never to trust a drunken man.

"A taxi for you," she said to Nikolai, pulling her cell phone out of her clutch.

From the foot of the bed where he made an adorably pretty picture, Nikolai stretched his leg and rubbed his leather boot against her bare calf. "Or we could spend the night here, Tina, *mi amore*. Now that things are truly over between you and the Greek thug—"

Using the tip of her stiletto, Tina poked his calf until he retreated with a very unmasculine squeal.

Her head was pounding. She'd barely drunk any water. Her body and mind were engaged in a boxing match over Kairos. The last thing she needed was Nikolai hitting on her.

"Kairos and I are not divorced. Also, I'm not interested in a relationship," she added for good measure.

"I noticed him tonight, *cara mia*. He spared you not a single glance." A claw against her heart. "As if you were total strangers." A bruise over her chest. "He seemed pretty interested in that whore Stella." Bile in her throat.

Just like a man to use the woman and then call her crude names. Oh, why had she come tonight? "*Per favore,* Nik, don't call her that."

"You called Claudia Vanderbilt much worse for marrying a sixty-year-old man."

Tina cringed, shame and regret washing over her like a cold wave.

She had.

She'd been privileged and pampered and had behaved so badly. She should keep Nikolai in her life. If nothing, he'd keep reminding her what a bitch she'd once been.

While Valentina held up her phone and walked around the bedroom looking for a signal—she'd spend the night here if it meant avoiding seeing Kairos leave with one of the women, not that he'd need to pay for the pleasure—Nikolai had moved closer.

Valentina froze when his hands landed on her hips. She arrested his questing hands. "Please,

Nikolai. I would like to keep the single friend I have."

"You have really changed, Tina. Transformed from a poisonous viper to a—" his alcoholic fumes invaded her nostrils while he tilted his head, seemingly in deep thought "—an innocent lamb? A lovely gazelle?"

Christo, the man was deeply drunk if he was calling her innocent.

Before Tina could shove Nikolai's hands away—she really didn't want to plant her knee in his groin like Luca had taught her—his hands were gone. Whether he skidded due to his drunken state or was pushed, Tina would never know. He landed with a soft thump against the bed, slid down it and let out a pathetic moan.

Tina whirled around, her breath hitching.

CHAPTER TWO

KAIROS STOOD AGAINST the back door, not a single hair out of place.

There was that stillness around him again, a stillness that seemed to contain passion and violence and emotion.

And yet nothing.

Emotions surged through her, like a wave cresting. But just like a wave broken by the strongest dam, Kairos had come pretty close to breaking her.

Ignoring the fact that her dress climbed up her thighs and she was probably flashing her thong at the inebriated Nikolai, she went to her knees next to him, sliding her fingers through his gelled hair.

Nikolai's hot, alcohol-laden breath fluttered over the expanse of her chest. But it was the silver gaze drilling holes into her back that pebbled goose bumps over her skin.

A sound like a swallowed curse emanated from

behind her. She ignored it, just as she tried to ignore her pounding heart.

"What are you doing?"

It had been nine months since she'd seen him. Nine months since he'd spoken to her. The hope that he would come after her had died after the first month. She swallowed to keep her voice steady. "Checking for a bump."

"Why?"

She snorted. "Because he's my friend and I care what happens to him."

Tina stared down at Nikolai's picture-pretty face and sighed. He *was* her friend.

He had gotten her the entry-level job in a fashion agency when she had returned to Milan from Paris, her tail tucked between her legs and ready to admit defeat, and found her a place with four other girls in a tiny one-bedroom hovel.

Not out of the generosity of his heart, but because he'd wanted to see her humiliated, wanted to enjoy how she'd come down in the world. Maybe even to get into her pants.

Whatever his motivations, Nikolai was the only one who'd helped her out, the only one who hadn't laughed at her pathetic attempts.

Unlike the man behind her, whose mocking

laugh even now pinged over her nerves. "You have no friends. At least not true ones. Shallow women flock to you for approval of their clothes and shoes. Men flock to you because they…"

Truth—every word was truth. Humiliating, wretched truth.

But it hurt. Like something heavy was pressing down on her chest. "Don't hold back now, Kairos," she said, smarting at the stinging behind her eyes.

"Because they assume that you'll be wild and fiery in bed. That you will bring all that passion and lack of self-control and that volatility to sex. Once your *friend* here gets what he wants, he will be through with you."

If she'd had any doubt what he thought of her, he'd just decimated it.

She had fallen in love with a man who thought she was good for sex and nothing else.

A need to claw back pounded through her. "I'm shallow and vapid, *si,* but what you see is what you get. I don't make false promises, Kairos."

The silence reverberated with his shock. "I've never made a promise to you that I didn't keep. I promised your brother to keep you in style when I agreed to marry you and I did. I promised you on the night of our engagement that I would show you pleasure unlike anything you've ever known and I believe I kept that promise."

I never said I loved you.

His unsaid statement hung in the air.

No…he hadn't said it. Not once.

It had all been her.

Stupid, naive Valentina building castles of love around this hard man.

She found no bump on Nikolai's thick skull and sighed with relief. His head lolling onto her chest, he fell asleep with an undignified snore. She'd have gagged at the sweat from Nikolai's flushed head trickling down her meager cleavage if all her reactions weren't attuned to the man behind her.

The small hairs on her neck stood up before Kairos spoke. "Leave him alone."

Ignoring him, she rose to her feet, and planted her hands under Nikolai's arms.

"Move, Valentina."

Before she could blink, Kairos hefted Nikolai up onto his shoulders and raised a brow at her.

He had carried her like that once, the hard muscles of his shoulders digging into her belly, his big hands wrapped around her upper thighs, after she had jumped into the pool at a business retreat in front of his colleagues and their wives because he'd ignored her all weekend.

He'd stripped her and thrown her into the cold shower, rage simmering in his eyes. And when he'd extracted her from the shower and rubbed her down, all that rage had converted into passion.

She'd been self-destructive just to get a rise out of him.

She looked away from the memory of that night in his eyes.

Masculine arrogance filled his eyes. "Now that the poor fool has served his purpose, shall I throw him overboard?"

"His purpose?"

"You used him to make me jealous—laughing at his jokes, dancing with him, touching him, to rile my temper. It is done, so you don't need him anymore."

"I told you, Nik is my friend." She jerked her gaze to his face and flushed. "And I did nothing tonight with you on my mind. My world doesn't revolve around you, Kairos. Not anymore." She wouldn't ask whether his temper was riled.

She wouldn't.

With a shrug, he dumped Nikolai on the bed like a sack of potatoes.

Nik's soft snores punctured the silence. If she weren't so caught up in the confusing cascade of emotions Kairos evoked, the whole thing would have been hilarious.

But nothing could cut through her awareness of six feet four inches of pure muscle and utter masculinity. She pressed her fingers to her temple. "Please leave now."

"Enough, Valentina. You've got my attention now. Tell me, did you really sign up with the escort service or was that just a dramatic touch to push me over the edge?"

"Are you asking me if I've been prostituting myself all these months?" She was proud of how steady she sounded while her heart thundered away in her chest.

"I thought perhaps no first. But knowing you and your vicious tendencies, who knows how far you went to shock me, to teach me a lesson, to bring me to heel?"

She walked to the door and held it for Kairos. "Get out."

He leaned against the foot of the bed, dwarfing

the room with his presence. "You're not staying here with him."

She folded her hands and tilted her head. The sheer breadth of his shoulders sucked the air from the room. "I've been doing *what* and *who* I want since the day I left you nine months ago, since I realized what a joke our marriage is. So it's a little late to play the possessive husband."

Hadn't she promised herself that she'd never stoop to provoking him like that again?

She cringed, closed her eyes at the dirty, inflammatory insinuation in her own words.

But she saw the imperceptible lick of fire in his gaze, the tiny flinch of that cruel upper lip. At one time, the little fracture in his control would have been a minor victory to her.

Not anymore.

"It is a good thing then, is it not, Valentina—" the way he said her name sent a curl of longing through her "—that I did not believe all your passionate avowals of love, *ne*?"

Something vibrated in the smooth calmness of his tone. The presence of that anger was a physical slap. Her eyes wide, she stared as he continued, his mouth taking on a cruel tilt.

"No more pathetic displays of your jealousy.

No grand declarations of love. No snarling at and slapping every woman I'm friends with. Now we both can work with each other on the same footing."

Dios, she'd always been a melodramatic fool. But Kairos, his inability to feel anything, his unwillingness to share a thought, an emotion…it had turned her into much worse. "*Non*, Kairos. No more of that," she agreed tiredly.

She didn't even have cash for a taxi, but if she'd learnt anything in the last nine months of this flailing about she'd been doing in the name of independence, it was that she could survive.

She could survive without designer clothes and shoes, she could survive without the adulation she'd taken as her due as the fashionista that Milan looked up to, she could survive without the Conti villa and the cars and the expensive lifestyle.

She picked up her clutch from the bed, her phone from the floor. "If you won't leave, I will."

He blocked the door with his shoulders. "Not dressed like a cheap hooker, strutting for business at dawn, you're not."

"I don't want—"

"I will throw you over my shoulder and lock you up in the stateroom."

It should have sounded dramatic, emotional. But Kairos didn't do drama. Didn't utter a word he didn't mean. *And if he so much as touched her...*

"Fine. Let's talk." She threw her clutch back on the bed and faced him. "Even better, why don't you call your lawyer and have him bring divorce papers? I'll sign them right now and we won't see each other ever again."

He didn't exactly startle. But again, Tina had the feeling that something in him became alert. She had...surprised him? Shocked him?

What did he think her leaving him had meant?

He stretched out his wrists, undid the cufflinks on his right hand—platinum cufflinks she'd bought him for their three-month anniversary with her brother's credit card—and pushed back the sleeve.

A shiver of anticipation curled around her spine.

He stretched his left hand toward her. Being left-handed, he'd always undone the right cuff link first. But the right hand...his fingers didn't do fine motor skills well. She'd noted it on their wedding night, how they had felt clumsy when he tried to do anything.

For a physically perfect specimen of masculinity, it had been a shock to note that the fingers of his right hand didn't work quite right. When she'd asked if he'd hurt his hand, he'd kissed her instead. The second time she'd asked, he'd just shrugged.

His usual response when he didn't want to talk.

She'd taken his left hand in hers and deftly undone the cufflink on their wedding night. And a thousand times after that.

It was one of a hundred rituals they'd had as man and wife. Such intimacy in a simple action. So much history in an everyday thing.

Tina stared at the blunt, square nails now, her breath ballooning up in her chest; the long fingers sprinkled with hair to the plain platinum band on his ring finger; the rough calluses on his palm because he didn't wear gloves when he lifted weights. It was a strong, powerful hand and yet when he touched her in the most sensitive places, it was capable of such feathery, tender movements.

A sheen of sweat coated every inch of her skin. *Dios*, she couldn't bear to touch him.

Without meeting his gaze, she took a few steps away from him. "What do I have to do to make you believe that I'm done with this marriage? That my behavior is not dictated anymore by trying to get you to acknowledge my existence?"

He smirked, noting the distance she'd put between them. "Is that what you did during our marriage?"

She leaned against the opposite wall and shrugged. "I want to talk about the divorce."

"You really want one?"

"*Si*. Whatever we had was not healthy and I don't want to live like that anymore."

"So Leandro enlightened you about the fat settlement you will receive then."

"What?"

"Your brother made sure you would receive a huge chunk of everything I own should we separate. Bloody insistent, if I remember correctly." His shrug highlighted those muscle-packed shoulders. "Maybe Leandro knew how hard you would make it for any man to stay married to you."

"You think that will hurt me? Leandro…" Her voice caught, the gulf she had put between her brothers and her a physical ache. "He practically raised me, he loved me when he could have hated me for our mother deserting him and Luca. And I still cut him out of my life because he thought so little of me that he had to bribe you to marry me. In the grand scheme of things that I've lost and learned, this marriage and anything I get by dissolving it…they mean nothing to me, Kairos."

He was upon her in the blink of an eye. The scent of him—a hint of male sweat and the mild thread of his cologne—hit her first. Awareness pooled low in her belly. He didn't touch her, and yet the heat of his body was a languid caress.

"How will you afford your haute couture and your designer stilettos then?"

"I haven't touched your credit cards in months. I haven't taken a single Euro from Leandro or Luca. Even the clothes I wear belong to Nikolai."

"Ah…" His gaze raked down the length of her body. The edge of cruelty in it stole her breath even as her skin tingled at his perusal. He nodded toward the happily snoring figure behind him on the bed. "Of course, your pimp dresses you now."

"Nikolai is not a pimp and he tricked me into believing tonight was just a party."

"I have to admit, only Valentina Constantinou could make a tacky, slinky dress look stylish and

sophisticated. But that skill is not really helping, is it? Paris chewed you out and threw you
back to Milan after a mere two months. Since
then, you've been licking the boots of everyone at
that fashion magazine. Fetching coffee for those
bitchy socialites, when you had once been their
queen bee, running errands in the rain for photographers and models that salivated over you for
years…" His gaze swept over her in that dismis-
sive way of his. "Have you had enough of reality?
Are you ready to return to your life of luxury?"

She wasn't surprised he knew what she'd been
up to in the last few months. "I don't care how
long it takes, I mean to—"

"Is that why you decided to try your hand at
the oldest profession in the world?"

"You're the one who bought me from Leandro,
remember? If anyone made me a whore, Kairos,
it was you." Every hurt she felt poured out into
her words, all her promises to herself to keep it
civil forgotten.

"I did not pursue you under false pretenses. I
did not take you to bed, hoping that a good per-
formance would bring me closer to the CEO position of the Conti board."

A blaze lit up in his silvery eyes, tight lines fanning around his mouth.

He tugged her and Tina fell onto him with a soft gasp. Hard muscles pushed against her breasts, sending shock waves through her. "Believe me, *pethi mou*, if there is one aspect of our marriage that both of us agree on, it is in bed."

His fingers wrapped around her nape in a possessive hold, a flicker of arousal and something else etched onto his features.

"You're the one who broke our marriage vows, Valentina. You're the one who avowed her love in passionate statements and sensational gestures, *ne*? Again and again. All I wanted was a civil marriage. Then, the fickle, spoilt brat that you are, you ran away because your little fantasy world where you rule as a queen and I fall at your feet crumbled. You leave no note. No message. You tell my security guard you're visiting your damned brothers. I imagined you kidnapped and waited for a ransom note. I imagined your body lying in some morgue because you met with an accident. I imagined one of the women or men you insulted with your cruel words may have been pushed to the limit and wrung your pretty neck."

Heart thundering, Valentina stared.

His fingers dug into her tender flesh with a grip she was sure would leave bruises. She'd never seen him like this, smoldering with a barely banked fire. "Until Leandro took pity on me and informed me that you had simply walked out on me. On our marriage."

Tina sagged against the wall, a strange twisting in her belly. He had been worried about her safety. *Terrified for her.* "I'm… I'm sorry. I didn't think…"

"Too little, too late."

He was right. If nothing else, he deserved an explanation. "I was furious with you and with Leandro. I had just learned that I was not a Conti but a bastard child my mother had with her chauffeur. That you married me as part of a bloody deal. You've had nine months to come after me." The words slipped past her tongue, desperate, pathetic.

And just like that, any emotion she had spied in his eyes was wiped away. He stared at his fingers pressing into her flesh, his other hand kneading her hip.

His eyes widened fractionally before he stepped back. Stopped touching her. "The moment Leandro informed me what you'd done, I stopped thinking of you. I had other matters—*urgent, important* matters—to deal with rather than chase my impulsive brat of a wife through Europe."

A fist to her heart would have been less painful.

But this was good, Tina reassured herself. She'd needed this talk with him. She'd needed to hear these words from Kairos's mouth. Now, she could stop wondering—in the middle of the night, alone in her bed—if she'd made a mistake.

If their marriage deserved another chance.

After tonight, she wouldn't have to see him again. Never hear those hateful words again. "*Bene.* You had important matters and I had enough time to think my decision through. I had nine months to realize what I did on impulse was right. I do not care whether you pay me alimony or not because I would not touch it. I intend to make something out of myself."

"By whoring yourself out to Russian investors? By dressing like a cheap tramp? Admit it, Valentina. You've gotten nowhere in nine months except ending up with that buffoon who wants to get in your pants. You have no talent. No skills. Your connections were the only things of value about you."

"I know that. Believe me, I have learned a life-time's worth of lessons in these nine months. The only good thing about this is that whatever connections you thought I would bring you as the Conti heiress are now lost."

"Your brothers haven't disowned you."

"I have cut all my connections with them. With that life. I'm of no more use to you."

"Ah...so that is your petty revenge? To deny what I planned to get by cutting yourself off from your brothers temporarily?"

"You give both me and your role in my life too much credit, Kairos. I love my brothers. Every day I spend away from them tears my heart. But it is the price I have to pay to face myself in the mirror."

Finally, it seemed that she was getting through to him. And still, ruthlessness was etched onto his every feature. "This marriage is not done until I say it is done."

"All I want is a teeny signature on a piece of paper. Ask me to sign away that alimony Leandro set up and I will. I will do anything you ask of me to be released from this marriage. You already wrote me out of your life when you decided not to come after me nine months ago, Kairos.

I was nothing but a disappointment to you. So why drag this on? Is it just because your masculine pride is dented? Is it because, once again, I made you lose your rigid self-control?"

"Whether you want it or not, whether you touch it or not, half of what is mine will be yours for years to come. If I'm going to pay through the nose for the mistake of indulging you in your foolish fantasies of everlasting love, for putting up with your temper tantrums, for the pleasure of having you in my bed, I would like three more months of marriage, *agapita*. And maybe, a little more of you for that price tag."

"A little more of me for that price..." Tina whispered, his words gouging through her already battered heart.

Her hand flew at him, outrage filling her every pore.

His lightning-fast reflexes didn't let her slap land. With a gentleness that belied the hard, wiry strength of his body, he held her wrist between them, crowding her body against the wall until it kissed the line of her spine.

Hardness and heat, he was so male. Her five-inch stilettos made up for the height difference between them until she was perfectly molded against him. Muscular thighs straddled hers. His granite chest grazed the tips of her breasts, making her nipples tighten and ache. And against her belly… *Maledizione*, his arousal was lengthening and hardening.

Damp heat uncurled between Tina's thighs. A whimper flew from her mouth—a needy and desperate plea for more. She clenched her thighs on instinct. "I do not even use my hands or my mouth. Yet you're damp and ready for me, *ne*?"

Breath shallow, she fought for control over her body, over the hunger he lit so easily. "As you said, it's why other men follow me around. I'm hot and uninhibited in bed, *si?* I could always match your sexual appetite and we both know it's insatiable. That I'm like a bitch in heat right now is not a point in your favor. You give good sex, Kairos. It was the one place where I was happy as your wife."

A lick of temper awakened in his silver eyes. "Tell me, Valentina. Do you get hot like this for any other man? For the fool lying in the bed behind us?" He twisted his hips in that way of his.

His erection rubbed against the lips of her sex and she jerked.

Pleasure was a fork in her spine, setting fire

along her nerves. She could feel that thick rigidness inside her, could see the tight control etched onto his features as he moved inside her. She craved the softening of his gaze, the few moments of the real Kairos, tender and caring, that she used to glimpse after he found his release.

And she still wanted that man. Like a puppy that had been kicked but still came back for more.

His mouth was at her cheekbone and his stubble chafed her lips. A wet, open kiss at her pulse. "I have other uses for you, wife…along with a few more months in my bed." His hands moved to cup her buttocks and pulled her against his hardness.

His mouth trailed lazily along her jawline, heading for her lips—the depth of her want, the fire along her skin—and she could taste the release in her fevered muscles.

"Admit defeat, Valentina. You can pretend all you want but your best bet is to be a rich man's trophy wife. It is not a bad role for you. Accept your limitations. Adjust your expectations. Just as I did when your brother Luca stood in the way of the Conti board CEO position. I want nothing more from a wife, and who knows? You can maybe even persuade me to give this marriage another try."

He *was angry* she had walked out.

No, not angry, she realized, running shaking hands through her hair.

He was furious with an icy, cold edge to it. Every word and caress of his was meant to provoke her with its cruelty. She'd never seen him like that.

It was more temper than she'd seen of him in all of their relationship so far—and, by God, she'd done every awful thing she could think of to provoke it.

But he wasn't asking her back. He didn't want to give their marriage another chance. He didn't want to give her a chance.

No, all he wanted was a sop to his male ego. All he wanted was to punish her for daring to leave him, for calling him out on his ruthless ambition.

That pain gave her a rope with which to climb out of the sensual haze. To deny herself what she'd never been able to before—his touch.

"Please, Kairos, release me."

The moment the words were out of her mouth, he let her go. Pupils drenched with lust, he stared at her as if he couldn't believe she could put a stop to it.

Shaking but determined to hold herself up, she met his gaze. "What do I have to do to get you to agree to a divorce? To get you to leave me alone?"

He looked taken aback but recovered fast. "Three months as my wife."

"Why? Why do you need me now? Other than because you want to punish me for walking out on you?"

"I have a debt to pay to Theseus."

"The man who brought you home from the streets, the one who adopted you?"

"*Ne.*"

"And for this, you need to have a wife?"

"Yes. His daughter Helena—"

"Is causing trouble between you and him? You want me to take her on? I don't understand how your wife's presence will help…" The words trailed away from her lips as she saw his closed off expression. A mocking laugh rose. "*Non*, I've got it, I think. The daughter wants you and you want to say no without hurting anyone's feelings. How noble of you, Kairos."

His brow cleared, relief dawning in his eyes. "Theseus deserves nothing less from me."

The depth of his sincerity shook Tina. She had never seen Kairos feel that strongly about anyone or anything. Except wealth and power and the amassing of it.

"This is the only way you get your divorce, Valentina."

"You cannot drag me back into that life against my will."

"But I can fight the divorce proceedings. Make your life into the media circus that you suddenly appear to abhor. And even worse, one wrong word or move from me toward you will bring forth your brothers' fury upon me and their interference in your life…if you truly intend to make it on your own, that would be hell."

Tina stared at him, amazed despite the anger pouring through her. He was calling her bluff about all this—the new direction she wanted to take in life.

She was damned if she answered it, damned if she didn't. She didn't want to spend another moment with him and yet he had left her no choice.

She sighed. "You will release me when things are clarified?"

"When things are clarified to *my* satisfaction, yes. No sooner. I'm warning you, Valentina, I want a perfect wife. No tantrums. No reckless escapades. You could even leave with the fat settlement the divorce will award you with the satisfaction that you've truly earned it. A novel feeling, I assure you."

"And if I sleep with you to earn it, you will have truly made me a whore, *si*, Kairos? Will your dented ego be repaired then? Because, hear me out, Kairos. My body might be willing but my heart is not."

The growl he swallowed down filled her with vicious satisfaction.

Valentina smiled for the first time in nine months.

Now all she'd have to do was convince herself of what she had told him.

CHAPTER THREE

WHAT DO I have to do to get you to leave me alone?

She truly wanted out of their marriage.

The realization moved through Kairos like an earthquake as he stared down at her sleeping form in the rear cabin of his private jet.

He'd only thought of how he would punish her when he found her. How good she would feel under him once again. How he would provoke her temper until she came at him all explosive fury and uncontained passion.

But she'd done nothing of the sort.

Oh, she'd lost control a couple of times and given him back as much as he'd deserved, but that was nothing to the Valentina he had known.

It was as if he was looking at a stranger.

If I sleep with you to earn it, you will have truly made me a whore.

Christos, only she could find such an appalling twist to what he had suggested.

But then since he was blackmailing her into his bed, was it any wonder that she had fought dirty?

He should have been impervious to her passionate, fiery declarations after ten months of living with her and her infamous tempers. Should have been unaffected by the sounds of her moans, the slide of her lithe body against his when he touched her.

That he wasn't, disconcerted him on a level he didn't understand.

His physical need for her and only her, and the fact that neither the sweet Stella nor any of the women who had readily offered him a place in their bed in the nine months since Valentina had walked out on him had remotely even tempted him, he could still somehow explain.

Like she had so crudely pointed out, Valentina was explosive in bed. He had been more than surprised when he'd discovered her virginity on their wedding night.

Valentina, as he'd quickly learned to his tremendous satisfaction, was an utterly sensual creature. Whatever he had taught her in bed, she'd not only taken to it enthusiastically but her innate curiosity for his body, her relentless eagerness to return every pleasure he had shown her. That she had remained untouched had been a shock.

She possessed a quick temper and an even quicker sexual trigger, and *Christos*, he'd reveled in making her explode to his slightest caresses. Tender and drawn-out, or explosive and fast, her passion had matched his own.

No man could be blamed for becoming obsessed like he had.

He needed Valentina with a fervor he didn't care or need to understand, and he would have her.

But the hurt in her eyes as he had dealt one cruel statement after the other, hoping to get her temper to rise, festered like an unhealed wound in the hours since he'd arranged for them to travel to Greece.

He should be grateful that the blinders were torn from her eyes. That she would not look at him anymore as if he were her knight in shining armor. Or the man who'd fulfilled all her romantic fantasies.

Whether they divorced or not, it was a good thing she had finally learned the truth.

He had no familiarity or place in his life for

tender feelings or love. They demanded a price he couldn't afford, however wealthy he had become.

But the sight of her huge brown eyes as he'd torn her into shreds with his words wouldn't leave him alone. He hadn't pulled any of his punches and she had taken them as if they were her due.

He didn't believe for a second that Valentina would stick to her chosen path or that she had what it took to succeed in her career.

She was just too undisciplined, too impulsive, too spoilt for the hard work it entailed. But still, for the first time in his life, Kairos felt as if he had stood up to the title that had haunted him all his childhood.

Bastard.

He was a bastard.

For even knowing that she would end up in his bed, even acknowledging that something intrinsic had changed in Valentina and he was the one who had caused it, knowing that he would hurt her, he still couldn't walk away from her.

Neither would he keep her.

For all that she'd professed her love for him, she had proved that she was like the rest—using love as manipulation, and then breaking her word.

No one was important enough for him to risk that, to forget the lesson he had already learned.

Love was nothing but a game.

For all your avowals, you left. You proved how little your words mean.

The words and the sentiment behind them stung Tina as she lathered up in the small shower cubicle.

Had there been an infinitesimal thread of complaint in Kairos's tone? Was she just reading too much when there was nothing again?

She had, at every available moment and opportunity, prostrated her feelings at his feet. Made a spectacle of herself.

How dare he think she'd given in too easily?

She wrapped a towel around herself, and stepped out.

Designer-label bags in every size and color covered the bed.

Mothership to Valentina... Calling now.

A soft sigh emerged from her lips.

She lasted nineteen seconds before she pulled the soft tissue out of the first bag and discovered a black cold-shoulder blouse and white capri pants. More casual pants and blouses. She counted four dresses ranging from a cocktail dress to a pale pink ball gown that would show off her tan beautifully.

Small, silky tissue bags of underwear and everything in her size. Makeup bags with her favorite lipsticks and perfumes with designer labels.

The bras were from the designer label she loved and sinfully expensive—two of them she had discovered recently would pay for her food for a month. And of the push-up kind she'd always preferred to make the most of her nonexistent boobage.

Sliding to the bed in her towel, Tina fingered the butter-soft cushioning of a push-up bra. In some throwaway remark he had made once when they'd watched an old Hollywood movie, she'd realized her husband had a thing for big breasts.

And hers were meager at best. So, like an idiot female, she'd gone on a rampage with lingerie, bras especially, and in the end there had been more cushioning and padding in her bra than flesh on her body.

One evening, she'd gone with an extreme push-up bra to a party—her boobs, exposed by a low neckline, almost kissing her chin and barely covering her nipples. Kairos had blown his top and called her entire outfit trampy—the first time in their marriage that he'd lost it.

He'd said, in clipped tones, that her need for every man's attention made her the shallowest woman he'd ever met. And then he'd walked out for the night.

She frowned.

For all his smarts, hadn't Kairos realized that she'd gone from one outrageous outfit to the next to get a rise out of him? To make up for what she thought she was lacking, for him? That from the moment Leandro had introduced her to him, she hadn't thought of another man ever again?

Why did she have to go to such extremes to please him?

Why was she even now, making such a big deal about the fact that he'd remembered the size of her underwear, of all things?

Kairos had a mind like a super computer, remembering every small detail that went in. It had no significance.

"A starved dog would look at meat scraps with less hunger," said a dry voice from the doorway.

Tina stood up and tugged the towel up.

He had also changed—a gray V-necked sweater that hugged his biceps and chest and dark jeans that caressed his muscular thighs. She had to swallow the feminine sigh of appreciation that wanted to come out.

"Old dogs can learn new tricks," she said repressively.

His laughter pervaded the small cabin. Grooves etched in his cheeks, his eyes alight with humor. "I think the saying says the opposite."

"I don't want the clothes."

"No choice. My wife, the fashionista of Milan, can't dress in trashy clothes that better suit a street walker or…" he picked up the worn-out denim shorts and loose T-shirt that she had put out "… hand-me-downs. Wow, you have really taken this role to heart, *ne*? You would have turned your nose up at these a few months ago."

"I would have, *si*. But it is not a joke, Kairos. Those are clothes that I could afford on what I made."

He threw the shirt carelessly aside. "You have to look the part, Valentina. Believe me, you're going to need the armor."

She frowned at the thoughtful look in his eyes. Armor for what? She'd been so caught up in staying strong against his onslaught she hadn't delved too much into the details. "I want to discuss this after I dress."

A brow raised, Kairos stared at her leisurely. Water drops clinging to her skin should burn and singe for the lazy intensity of his gaze. "Still so modest, Valentina? I have seen, touched, licked, sucked every part of you, *ne*?"

She glared at him. "I was willing then. Not anymore."

"But I can see you if I close my eyes." He closed his eyes, leaning against the wall. A wicked smile dancing around his lips. "The mole on the curve of your right buttock. The mark you have on your knee from skinning it. The silky folds of—"

She pressed her palm to his mouth and whispered, "Stop, please."

Unholy humor glinted in his silver eyes. "That's not all. I have the sounds you make, the way you thrust your hips up when I'm deep inside you, I have them all in my head." He tapped his temple, his nostrils flaring. "They're the first things I recall in the morning when I wake up with—"

She drew her hand back, burned. But even beneath the sensual web around them, it was the humor in his eyes that threw her. "You're shameless."

His eyes followed a drop of water from her neck to the tight cinch of her towel. A devilish smile glinted around his mouth. "You know how I get in the morning, *ne*? You left me with no recourse." He pulled up her left hand and frowned. "Where are your rings?"

"In my bag."

With purposeful movements, he looked through her bag. Stalking back to her, he pushed the rings on her finger. Another sleek box appeared from somewhere.

Her heart thundered as he pulled out a simple gold chain with a diamond pendant.

The pendant was a thumbnail sized V in delicately twisted platinum and gold with tiny diamonds lining up the branches. She had seen it at a jewelry store once—on one rare occasion when they'd been out shopping together to buy a gift for her niece Izzie. Buying it with her credit card—against Kairos's dictate that she stop spending Leandro's money—would have been easy.

But already…something had changed in her back then.

Clothes and shoes and jewelry had begun to lose their allure. Because none of those, she had realized, made a difference in how her reserved husband saw her.

And yet he'd noticed her watching it.

She met his eyes over the fragile chain dangling in his fingers. "I… I have a lot of funky jewelry to dress the part. I can't stand the thought of fake gifts."

"I bought it for you. We might as well use it." With one hand, he pushed the swathe of her hair aside, then his hands were gentle around her neck. His warm breath feathered over her face, his arms a languorous weight over her shoulders. "Throw it away after we're done with this for all I care."

The pendant was cold against her bare skin. Tina licked her lips, warmth pooling in her chest. "When?"

His fingers lingered over the nape of her neck, straightening the chain, but still her heart went thud against her ribcage. "When what?"

"When did you buy it?"

"When you were waiting outside, in the car. I meant to give it to you on—" he laughed, and yet beneath the mockery Tina sensed self-deprecation, even anger "—the ten-month anniversary of our wedding. I feel like a fool even saying that."

"Then why did you buy it?" Her tummy rolled at his proximity, at the revelation. "You called me a sentimental little fool when I bought you gifts on that date. A child who celebrates every little thing."

"Maybe you finally wore me down. But then you left two days after that shopping trip, so maybe it's a good thing I didn't change too much for you, *ne*?" he said, looking away.

This time, there was no doubt that he was angry, even bitter that she had left him. That she had given up on their marriage. She must have changed him a little if he had truly thought of giving her a gift on that date. Maybe just a little.

But still, he hadn't acted on that anger. He had simply written her off, like a bad asset. He had only come for her when he decided he needed her. She had to remember that.

"The clothes, the shoes, everything will stay." He walked away, a faint tension radiating from him. "I want the classy, stylish Valentina. The adoring, loving wife."

"I can't force the last part."

"Pretend then. For months, you did just that anyway. Do you need anything else?"

"Underwear. Bras, to be exact," she said the first thing that came to her lips while her mind whirled. Had he cared about her just a little? Had he bought her the necklace to make her happy?

Did his humiliating proposal that she could persuade him to try again hold a hint of what he wanted?

"The ones I have are plain cotton and will show—"

"Things I'd rather not have anyone but me see in those slinky dresses," he finished for her, possessiveness ringing in his tone. He frowned and looked at the reams of new bras. "I had my PA order those from the boutique you spend a fortune in."

She sighed—she really did like how big those push-up bras made her breasts look. No, what she liked was that they had made her feel like he would like her more. But no more of her crazy shenanigans. "Those don't…fit anymore."

His gaze moved to her chest like a laser beam. The wicked devil! "I can't tell from under that towel."

She picked up a pen and notepad and wrote down her size.

"No underwire, no padding, no lifting. All you're going to get is my tiny boobs as nature made them," she muttered to herself.

He laughed, half choking on it. She jerked her head up, realizing too late he'd been standing far too close. He stared at her as if she had grown two horns. "What?"

She pasted a fake smile to her lips. "My sanity returned nine months ago. I can't wait for the next three months to be over."

He scowled. Didn't even bother to hide it.

"Fortunately, I know you well enough not to trust a word out of your lovely mouth," said the blasted man.

If a shiver claimed her spine, she didn't let it show on her face.

A few more months in my bed...

A rich man's trophy wife...

Kairos would never see her as anything else.

She'd seen how he behaved with her sister-in-law Sophia, one of his oldest friends. A woman he'd proposed to before he'd decided on Tina herself.

Sophia was the smartest woman Tina knew.

And she commanded Kairos's respect. Even Leandro's wife Alexis had Kairos's regard.

Both women, so different, and yet they had one thing in common that she did not have.

They were successful in their own right—strong, independent women who were more than enough to take on her powerful brothers Leandro and Luca.

That was what Tina wanted to be. That was what she wanted to see in his eyes when he looked at her.

If he was going to tease and torment her for three months, then she would earn his respect, his regard. She was Valentina Conti Constantinou and she would have her own form of revenge by succeeding beyond his wildest dreams.

She would rub his face in what he was giving up. And only then, only when she had brought him to his knees, would Valentina walk away. Even her Machiavellian grandfather Antonio, who'd only ever accepted her under pressure from Leandro, couldn't deny that she was any less of a scheming Conti now.

She turned around and faced Kairos. "I have been thinking of our deal since last night."

Steady, flat, her voice cooperated. "I have a few conditions."

His nostrils flared. "You don't get to negotiate."

That she had shocked him snapped her spine into place.

She let a smile curve her mouth. She hadn't been born a Conti, but her proud, powerful brothers had raised her to be one. "I might be vain and vapid but I'm not *stupido*, Kairos. You came to me last night because you need me. So, *si*, I will negotiate and you will listen."

"What are your conditions?"

"You were right about the industry being a bitch. I didn't get anywhere in nine months. I want word spread that we're back together again. I want the names and numbers of everyone you do business with. And I want your backing."

"I'm a respected businessman, Valentina. I will not give the weight of my name to any harebrained scheme of yours that is sure to embarrass me and sink in a few months. If you want my money, you have to wait until the divorce is final to get your hands on it."

"*Non*! Not money. I want access to your rich friends and their wives. Or their mistresses. I don't care how you put it forward. Tell them your juvenile, impulsive bratty wife is putting together a shoot and you're indulging her. Tell them it's the way I'm whiling away my useless life. Tell them it's your way of indulging my tantrums. I don't care what you tell them. I need to put together a portfolio and a shoot. I need to get word of mouth going that I'm offering my services as a personal stylist to anyone who's got reputation, status and money."

"A personal stylist?"

"*Si.*" She raised her hand, cutting him off. "If you're going to use me, Kairos, I will use you, too. At least, we're finally speaking the same language."

"And what language is that, Valentina?"

"The language of transactions. You never do anything without some advantage to yourself. Our marriage has taught me one useful thing at least."

"You're playing a dangerous game, *pethi mou,* hurling accusations at me. You can only push me so far."

"I know you'll find it hard to believe, but I'm not doing anything to provoke you, Kairos. For the first time in my life, I'm thinking with my head. I've looked past the surface and not liked what I see in myself.

You have made me face reality. And for that, I shall always be grateful to you."

"You want a divorce because you're grateful to me?" The stony mask of his face belied how angry he was with her again. No, not anger. But he was affected by her decision.

"Just because I've realized what was wrong with me doesn't mean you were right, does it? I will never give you power over me again."

For all her brazen confidence, she'd never stripped before him, because she had thought her body imperfect, not made to his specifications and preferences.

Or maybe because she had always wanted to be perfect to please him—perfect straight hair, perfect dress, perfect posture.

It had got her exactly nowhere with him.

Without waiting for his response, her breath suspended in her throat, she picked some underwear. Her back to him, she dropped the towel. The soft exhale behind her pulled her nerves taut. Somehow, she managed to pull her panties up the right way and hooked her bra on.

The intensity of his gaze on her body burned

over her skin, as if he was stroking it with those clever fingers. But she was determined to see this through, to prove to him that he wouldn't always have the upper hand.

With barely a glance in his direction, she pulled on a pair of capri pants and a white silk top.

And then, head held high, she walked out to the main cabin, her heart a deafening roar in her chest.

She was tweaking the tiger's tail, true. But she had to do this. She had to prove to him that she was made of stronger stuff. And then, when the three months were up, she would have his respect and then she would walk away.

CHAPTER FOUR

THEY ARRIVED AT a large estate on the island of Mykonos around six in the evening in a tinted limo.

A grove of dark green olive trees beckoned as the car drove up the curving driveway.

Lush green surrounded the whitewashed villa nestled in a picturesque setting. Blue beaches stretched as far as the eye could see.

But Tina barely took it in for her gaze stuck to the myriad expressions crossing her husband's usually expressionless face.

His chest had risen and fallen with a deep breath at the first sight of the villa. His jaw clenched tight at the sight of a green sports model Beetle. Tenderness and ache and grim determination flashed across his silver eyes at the sight of the three people—an older man and woman and a young woman—waiting at the top of the steps.

Tina felt as if she was standing in a minefield.

She'd never seen Kairos show so much emotion, much less such varying reactions.

"Kairos?" she said softly, loath to disturb the glimpse she was getting into a man she'd thought felt nothing, held nothing sacred.

His gaze turned to her from the opposite seat. And in the seconds it took him to focus on her, his expression became blank, as easily as if he'd donned a mask, completely shutting her out yet again.

But she couldn't scream or fight him for his usual response. "What exactly does this debt to Theseus entail, Kairos?"

Hesitation like she'd never seen flickered across his face. "There are some duties I need to fulfill. That's all you need to know."

Curiosity ate through Tina even as she told herself to stay out of it.

In ten months of marriage, all she'd learned about him was that he was an orphan who had grown up on the streets of Athens. That he had had a mentor who had given him an education. That was it, no more.

Getting her husband to talk about himself, his past, or his emotions was like getting blood out of stone. She'd honestly never met a man who talked so little.

Something about the tension wreathed in his face made her say, "You're not going to murder someone and ask me to lie for you in court, are you?"

His mouth twitched. "So you haven't stopped watching American soap operas."

"Sell me to land a business deal like that guy did in *Indecent Proposal*?"

He laughed. The warm sound enveloped her in the dark interior.

"*Oxhi*... No," he clarified. "Even if I wanted to, I don't think there's a man living who'd know how to handle you, Valentina."

"I know *oxhi* means no," she said, trying to think of his statement as a compliment. "I plan to say it quite a lot to you over the next few months. In English, Italian *and* Greek," she added for good measure.

Memories permeated the air between them, bringing a smile to her own lips.

For the first month of their marriage, they had had hilarious moments, teaching each other Italian and Greek. But they had both settled on English in the end.

Except when he made love to her. Then he slipped into Greek—guttural, pithy words that even now sent a shiver through her insides. Words she'd never hear again.

No, words she didn't want to hear, she clarified for herself.

"Cold?" he asked, his head dipping down toward her as she exited the car.

She shook her head but he draped a muscled arm around her shoulders, pulling her flush against his side. A clamor of sensation rose inside her. But still, she was aware of a pair of eyes drilling holes into her.

The younger woman, she knew instinctually.

A sliver of apprehension clamped her spine. "Kairos, this feels—"

He cut her off with the press of his lips.

It began as a soft nuzzle. A tender hold of her jaw. A warning to play along in his eyes. Barely a slide of his body against hers.

A show. He was putting on a show. For that woman, Helena.

And yet, as their lips met, as her chest grazed his, as his hand descended to her hip to keep her steady, everything changed.

Nine months of deprivation came pouring out. Desire rose—swift and spiraling.

Heat and pleasure radiated from where their lips grazed and pressed. Air left her lungs. Her knees wobbled and she clutched his arm. A whimper fell from her mouth when he licked the seam of her lips.

He cursed against her lips and Tina instantly opened up. The masterful glide of his tongue against hers made her moan and press harder into his hard body. Her hands crawled to the nape of his neck, her fingers pushing into his rough hair.

The world around them dissolved. Colors burned behind her eyelids, desire making her blood heavy. She could feel the defined contours of his body digging into hers. Images and sensations from memory drowned the little thread of her will: the cradle of his hard hips bearing her down into the mattress; his rock-hard thighs pushing against the soft flesh of hers; the utterly masculine grunt at the back of his throat when she dug her nails into his back.

Heat bloomed low in her belly as he swept over every inch of her mouth with glorious, knowing strokes. No tenderness. No holding back.

Purely carnal, he thrust in and out of her mouth with his tongue.

Pockets of heat erupted all over her, her clothes caging the sensations against her hot skin.

One hand around her neck and one encircling her hip, he held her the way he needed for his onslaught, only letting her come up for air briefly before he claimed her mouth again. He bit her lower lip with such aggressive possession that she moaned. Pleasure and pain wound around her senses.

Instantly he gentled the kiss, laving the hurt with his tongue.

Softer and slower. Ache upon ache built in her lower belly, spinning and spiraling. Tina whimpered against his mouth, craving release. Craving this closeness with him.

"Enough, Kairos! Introduce us to your little plaything."

The venom in that voice, hidden beneath a vein of sweet playfulness, was ice water over Tina's head. She pulled away, heart thundering a million miles an hour in her ears. Her lips stung, her entire body thrummed with need.

"Helena, please be…polite," came another soft voice.

His fingertips trailing lazily against her jawline, his chest rising and falling, Kairos let out a soft growl that reverberated along her trembling body. Tina sensed his shock as her own senses began to clear.

"Nine months..." he whispered against her mouth, his forehead touching hers in uncharacteristic affection. "Even if I hadn't needed you here for this day, *pethi mou*... You and I are not through."

The words were feral. Possessive. And not meant for their audience.

Tina licked her lips and tasted him there. But all he meant was for sex, she reminded her sinking senses. She frowned. "It is just one kiss."

Masculine arrogance etched into every line of his face. "You will come to me, *pethi mou*. I simply shall not allow it to be otherwise." He rubbed her lips with the pad of his thumb. "I might, however, decide not to give you what you want. As a punishment."

She saw it now. He meant to use these months to work her out of his system. He didn't like it that he still wanted her so much. And then, he would walk away.

And if the kiss had been any indication, he was

right. She hadn't even mustered a token protest. "This is a game to you, isn't it? Like who will blink first, or who will draw first and shoot the other person?"

"You're the one who always plays games."

Anger and frustration pulsed through her. "No more," she said, tilting her head toward the woman waiting. She rubbed at a piece of nonexistent lint on his shirt, felt the thundering of his heart under her palm. "My days of fighting for you are over, Kairos. That woman and you are welcome to each other."

"I have never loved you, Valentina. When we were married, I could barely stand your theatrics and tantrums. But believe me when I say the only woman I have desired since I met you, the only woman that drives me insane with lust, is you. I want only you, *glykia mou*."

The truth of his declaration reverberated through Tina, leaving her shaking. His own disbelief that he still wanted her, his frustration at his inability to understand it, much less control it, saturated his words.

She barely processed it—four sentences about what he felt or didn't feel from Kairos was like a long speech from any other man—before she felt the younger woman right behind them. Her subtle floral perfume carried to them on the air.

His shoulders tensing, Kairos moved them toward the couple who had come down the stairs but who waited at a discreet distance. His arm remained at her waist in a possessive grip.

"Valentina, this is Theseus Markos and his wife Maria. They are—" his Adam's Apple bobbed as he hesitated "—friends of mine." Tension built in the older couple's faces at his label. Jaw tight, he nodded to the younger woman. "And this is their daughter Helena. My wife, Valentina Constantinou." Possession was imbued in the softly spoken words.

He addressed the greeting mainly to the man.

With a head full of thick gray hair, Theseus looked to be in his sixties. He had a heavy, beefy build but even in the afternoon sun there was an unhealthy pallor to his skin. As if he had spent the last few months away from it.

Tina shook his hand, which was warm beneath her fingers. "We have been very curious about you, Valentina," he said genuinely, the wariness melting from his gaze. Unlike Kairos, his accent was thick. "Welcome to our home. We hope you are not angry with us for taking your husband away from you for so long. Kairos has been an immense help here."

"Of course I'm not," Tina said as if she knew all about it.

This was her chance to dig in and ask questions. True to her self-centered mindset, she had simply assumed that Kairos had been away because he hadn't cared about her fleeing their marriage.

But knowing that he had been here in Greece where his presence was needed and appreciated so much, changed her view.

Maria Markos was more subdued in her welcome, though no less honest. She seemed…anxious and distracted.

Tina thanked them for their welcome.

Only then did she allow herself to look at the woman standing at the periphery. She was a striking contrast to her parents—in both health and attitude. And older than Kairos's twenty-nine.

Thick, wavy black hair was expertly styled around contrastingly waif-like features. A pale yellow sleeveless dress hugged every inch of her big breasts and tiny waist, and fell to above her knees. Familiar with the latest fashions, Valentina instantly noted the designer of that dress and the three-inch wedge platforms she wore. A simple gold necklace with a big diamond pendant shone at her neck. As did matching diamond studs at her ears.

She was short and voluptuous, almost overflowing out of her dress.

Instead of meeting Tina's eyes, Helena threw herself at Kairos. Kairos didn't let his displeasure show, but it was there all the same in the tightness of his mouth, in the way he immediately bowed his body so that only their shoulders touched.

She shouldn't have required the evidence after his statement. Yet, something in her calmed to see that he didn't want nor welcome Helena's attention.

Neither did the woman miss it. She still kissed his cheek, and squeezed his biceps, with a long-drawn sigh, as if she were welcoming a long-lost lover home.

Tina looked at Helena's parents and saw their discomfiture at their daughter's unseemly display toward Kairos in front of his wife. She cringed.

Hadn't she behaved just like Helena at one time?

Becoming jealous and irrational every time

Kairos had spent one-on-one time with another woman? Hadn't she tried to stake her claim over him—just as Helena had just done—in a party full of guests, because she'd been insecure and impulsive?

Dear lord, she'd slapped her now sister-in-law because she'd learned of Kairos's regard for her. Thankfully, Sophia had been kind, seeing Tina's insecurity and had befriended her despite her awful behavior.

The outline of Helena's lipstick on Kairos's cheek called to her now, invoking her rash temper, that possessive urge to show that he belonged to her. And only her.

She trembled from the will it took to control herself.

Fortunately, before she could make a fool of herself, Theseus claimed Kairos's attention and Maria followed them up the stairs.

The silence became fraught as Helena stared at her openly. There was no overt animosity in her stare, yet it was all there.

"Valentina Conti Constantinou," Helena said her name with a flourish, ignoring the hand Tina offered. "Although the Conti is apparently not quite true, *ne*?" She didn't wait for Tina to reply.

"Poor Kairos. He assumed he was getting the rich Conti heiress, and instead ended up with…a talentless, fortuneless hack. I have heard that even your powerful Conti brothers have deserted you. I wonder why, after all these months, he brings you back into his life."

It shouldn't have hurt. She'd heard the same from countless mouths, people she'd considered friends, who had assumed the same of her situation and his actions innumerable times.

Hearing that Kairos had ended up with a talentless, poor, bastard of a wife—and that it was *her*—hurt like a piece of glass through her flesh.

Because it was all true. It was what she thought about herself in the worst moments.

She'd never taken a fight lying down but no words came. Like the little girl she'd once been, grieving for her mother, she wished her brothers were here, that she had Leandro's arms to cocoon her in safety, that Luca was at her back bucking her up, that more than anything she had the respect and trust of the man she had once loved so desperately to throw back in the spiteful woman's face.

But she had none of them around her. She had nothing but the truth to face.

Swallowing the deep ache in her belly, she considered the woman staring at her.

Again, she saw the similarities between her and Helena. The insecurity beneath the beauty, the expensive clothes and shoes, the pampered, spoilt attitude that screamed that what she wanted, she would have.

But neither did she feel sympathy for Helena. "Maybe Kairos realized that even without all the trappings of wealth and fortune, he still wants me. He needs me desperately." Just saying the false words was a punch to her middle.

As if she hadn't spewed the most hateful things to her face, Helena looped her arm through Tina's and propelled her forward. "In the end, he will discard you again, you know. He will choose me. We have too much history between us. It would be better for you if you accept that."

"What history?" The question escaped her mouth before Tina could bury it forever.

Helena laughed. A gentle, tinkling sound. "He hasn't told you? Then I can't, either."

With a smile, she wandered off, leaving Tina at the entrance, wondering at the sanity of the woman. And her own, as well.

What the hell had Kairos dropped her in the

midst of? What was it that he wanted of her? To scratch and scream at the woman who so boldly touched her husband in front of her? And if she did, how much would be for pretense and how much for real?

Unless he did want to win Helena's hand in the end and was only using Tina to make her jealous, to cement his grip over Helena? To get a better deal?

Bile crawled up her throat.

No! She wasn't going to torture herself like this.

He was welcome to the woman, if that was what he really wanted.

Her skin prickling, she looked up.

Kairos was standing at the balcony with a wine glass in his hand, studying her openly while Theseus talked to him from the side. His shirt was undone at the cuffs and to his chest, owing to the summer heat. The sun glinted off the dial of his platinum watch—her six-month anniversary gift to him, bought with Leandro's money.

That he had kept the watch didn't mean anything. All the thousand tiny things didn't mean anything when he hadn't come for her.

It was her mantra.

He raised the wine glass to her in a mocking toast, his brows raised inquiringly.

She knew what he could see in her face—her longing for him, her distress that he might want Helena, her frustration that he still had this much power over her.

She chased away every expression from her face. Took a deep breath. Even affixed a smile to her mouth.

She pulled her phone from her clutch and texted him, then waited for him to see her text.

The shock in his gaze, the smile fighting to emerge around his mouth…it was a balm to her soul.

Shocking Kairos was her barometer in her fight for independence and if him raising his wine-glass to salute her was any indication, she had won this round.

CHAPTER FIVE

*Your move, Kairos...keep up your side of the
bargain.*

LIKE A LOVESICK teenager, Kairos stared at Valentina's text for the millionth time since the night
they had arrived. Like she used to say when he
had taught her chess.

True to form, he was a master at strategizing,
never betraying himself with a look or gesture,
laying out traps to lure her in. And she, impulsive, bloodthirsty and eager for mayhem, would
charge forward with everything she had, would
mount attacks without thinking them through
and had always walked into his traps.

It had been a delight to teach her, to see her
fight her innate nature and try to stay at least one
step ahead of him.

But yesterday, the week since he had seen her
on the yacht had been nothing like guessing her

chess strategy. The woman he had married was nothing if not unpredictable.

He'd expected her to throw a tantrum right in front of the steps when Helena had hugged him and kissed him in a provoking display. Helena's actions had been purely for Valentina's and Theseus's benefit.

And yet Valentina had recovered. Quickly and smoothly. Had kept her composure as he'd never seen her do before.

And there had been no questions. At all. About his past. About his past relationship with Helena. About his history with Theseus and Maria.

Nothing.

He'd seen her during dinner, then kissed her cheek good-night. Like the quiet, poised wife he'd always wanted, she'd retired without a word at the appropriate time. When he had finally gone to bed around midnight, she'd been asleep.

When he'd gone outside at five the next morning for his run, he had found her running laps around the house already. When he'd quietly joined her, she'd barely blinked.

It had been the same for four days. Since he'd been gone for more than a week to fetch her, work had piled up. So he had left her mostly in

Maria's care, knowing that she would treat Valentina with kindness, at the least.

Even as he wondered how long this new serenity would last, he missed the Valentina he'd married. The Valentina that had given voice to every feeling that had crossed her mind, the Valentina that lived through every emotion fearlessly, the Valentina that had, again and again, vowed that she'd always love him.

The Valentina that he only realized after she had left him had brought so much color and noise to his life.

The realization unsettled him.

Designer clothes, haute couture heels and reigning over her little clique—that had been the extent of her interests.

You have made me face reality, she had claimed.

And the weight of that statement hung around his neck. He hadn't wanted the weight of her love nine months ago and he didn't want the burden of the new direction her life had taken now, either.

Attachment and affection only brought the worst out in all people, as Theseus had taught him seven years ago. And Kairos never wanted to experience the pain that came from people letting him down. Of people taking away what they had given, when it was not convenient anymore.

But of course, all this was dependent on the fact that Valentina had changed. And *that* he still could not believe.

Just as he was about to check where she was, Valentina walked into the sunlit breakfast room.

Desire punched him anew, a sharp pulse of longing that he didn't quite understand beneath the voracious hunger.

She stilled at the buffet laid out on the side table, like a doe caught in the sights of a predator. Slowly, her breath evened out, her expression assuming that calm he was beginning to detest.

There were a lot of changes in his wife and this was the most aggravating. She'd never been able to hide her emotions before. *Christos*, there'd been moments when her open longing for him had embarrassed him, when he'd wished she had a little control over herself.

Only now, when he couldn't decipher what was running through her mind, did he appreciate how refreshingly guileless and unflinchingly honest she had been. Only now when she was scrunched up in a corner of the bed did he realize how much he'd missed her warmth in his bed.

"*Kalimera*, Valentina," he said, his tone husky.

"*Buongiorno*, Kairos," she greeted sharply, and turned away toward the food.

He didn't drop his gaze from the delectable picture she made. The tight clench of her shoulders covered in thin straps told him she was aware of his gaze.

Black trousers followed the line of her long legs lovingly—legs that she had wrapped around his shoulders more than once. An emerald green blouse showed off her toned arms.

The wide V-neck gave no hint of a cleavage—had she finally abandoned those ghastly bras that had hidden the curve of her soft flesh from his fingers but exposed the bones in her chest?

She had always been more muscled than soft or fleshy because of her runner's build but she bordered on scrawny now. Even last night, as she had cozied up to him unknowingly in sleep, he had noted she was all sharp angles and bones. Not that it had made any difference to the erection he had sported in a matter of seconds. It was as if he had no control over his lust when it came to her. Lust he needed to address soon.

She had fashioned her glorious hair into some

kind of tight braid, pulling it away from her face. It only made her features sharper.

He frowned at her grapefruit and coffee. And the way she settled down at the chair farthest from his. "You have lost weight."

She shrugged, raising those bony shoulders. "I didn't eat much in the last few months."

"Or sleep much?" The dark shadows under her expressive brown eyes were still there after a week. "You missed me so much that you couldn't eat and sleep?" he said, wanting to see a smile on her lips. Wanting that wariness in her eyes gone.

"I didn't know you were capable of cracking a joke," she taunted. Then sighed. "I would think you wouldn't want to engage in a discussion about our marriage where Theseus or his family could walk in or overhear."

"Theseus took Maria and Helena out first thing in the morning for a tour of the estate as it's Saturday. To give us the privacy we've been denied for the past week."

"That was kind of him," she replied. "Is he well? He looks like my grandfather—" she shook her head, a raw glitter in her eyes "—like Antonio did after his heart attack."

A tightness gathered in his chest at the clear

distress in her gaze. "Antonio said words to you about your mother?" He knew how much importance the Conti patriarch put on his bloodline.

"He didn't dare say a thing to me. Not in front of Leandro and Luca." The flat tone in which she spoke revealed how much it really did matter to her. "But I finally realized why he'd always been reserved with me. I always wondered if it were the fact that I was a girl that he cared so little for me.

"Now I know it's because I'm not really his blood." She pushed a lock of hair behind her ear. "Tell me about Theseus."

Why did her pain reach him like a hand into his chest when nothing she'd ever done had? Because he'd never even thought her capable of this depth? Kairos cleared his throat. He didn't know how to handle her emotion. Or maybe he didn't know how to handle this new Valentina at all.

"Theseus had a heart attack nine months ago. Maria says his health had been suffering for a while. An almost successful hostile takeover at his company, I think, precipitated the attack. For a while there, we weren't sure he'd make it through."

"He sent for you then?"

"Something like that."

"You've been here all these months?"

"Yes."

"And the hostile takeover?"

"I stopped it."

"He thinks the world of you, doesn't he?"

He shrugged. "Doesn't matter what he thinks. I…have a duty to him, that's all."

Kairos waited for a question about Helena to come his way. He waited for the cloak of zen around her to disappear now that she knew they'd have no audience.

Time ticked on, seconds gathering into minutes. Only silence.

Disappointment curdled in his stomach.

She took a sip of her coffee. "I…wasn't making enough to buy nice meals and afford the rent on the flat," she said, answering his earlier comment. "Even shared four ways, it was steep."

Her guilelessness in openly admitting failure after he had taunted her shamed him. Scraped him raw, too. "Was it so awful to remain married to me that you preferred walking away from every luxury I offered? From the penthouse suite and an unlimited credit card to live in some hovel with three other women and barely enough to eat?"

"*Si,* it was."

Blunt, and without the theatrics. Everything about this...*new her* unsettled him.

"I'm to believe that neither of your overprotective brothers smothered you in money and comforts? Not even a care package from Luca?"

"Luca respects my wishes. Leandro..." Her throat moved, her knuckles tight around her coffee cup.

Longing vibrated in her voice. This—this rift with her brothers, obviously enforced by her, more than anything else made him wonder about the change in her.

Leandro, Luca and Valentina shared a bond unlike anything he'd ever seen before. Even more astonishing, for it had been revealed that Valentina only shared a mother with her brothers.

Was that why he had gravitated toward Leandro's offer when there had been so many?

No, he hadn't been looking for a ready-made family. He had been burned enough with the one he had considered his.

It was Valentina that had caught his attention from the first moment Leandro had pointed her out to him. Valentina whom he had wanted to possess.

She rose, put away her untouched grapefruit. "I told Leandro our rift will be permanent if he interferes in my life again."

That she meant it was clear. That it tore at her was also clear.

He had wished so many times that she was more intellectual, more contained...more everything she was not. Yet now that she was like a shadow of her former self, he felt protective of her. "You barely ate anything."

"Since when do you—"

He watched, fascinated, as she shook her head, took a deep breath that made her chest rise invitingly and then met his gaze. "I want to talk about what you're going to do for me. I made a list of—"

"I can do a lot of things for you, Valentina, if only you'd quit this whole 'Independent Valentina' project."

"Wow! Jokes and innuendoes, I don't know if you're the Kairos I married or not. All I usually got were nods and sighs and grunts. And oh, that look you used to get when you wanted sex."

Seeing Kairos disconcerted was like an adrenaline shot to her body.

Dark color stole under his cheeks and for the first time in months, Valentina laughed.

He pushed his chair back and stretched his long legs. His running shorts pulled back, exposing the hard muscle of his thighs. Greedily, she drank in the hair-roughened legs, and the calves. Her breath halted in her throat. Until she'd seen Kairos's muscled calves, she hadn't thought of a man's calves as sexually arousing.

But then, every inch of him was made to be appreciated. Touched. Stroked. Licked…not that he'd ever given her a chance to do all those things. Even in that arena, he had held the strings.

"I don't know what you're talking about." His words tugged her out of the sensual haze. "In my defense, you usually talked so much, fought so much, bitched so much that all I could interject was nods and grunts."

Even his cruel remark couldn't dampen her spirits. "You would get this strange glitter in your eyes. First, you would fight it. As if wanting to sleep with your wife was an urge you had to conquer. Then a run, followed by a shower. Then you would walk into our bedroom and stare at me. For a while there, I thought you found my pajamas distasteful. Then you—"

"You thought I found those little shorts with bows on the sides and sleeveless, braless tops you wore distasteful?"

"You'd sit in the chaise, elbows on your knees, and rub your neck," Tina continued as if his words hadn't sent a shiver of pleasure down her spine. "If you ran your fingers through your hair three times, I knew I was going to get laid that night. If you swore during all this aforementioned waiting time, it meant…"

Stillness surrounded him. Dark slashes of color in his cheeks. "It meant what?"

"Never mind," she dodged.

"What did it mean, Valentina?"

"It meant you would be demanding and a little…rough. It meant you would draw it out until I had no breath left in me. Until I was begging for you to grant me release."

It meant he would punish her. For his own loss of self-control as he saw it. For pushing him to the edge, Tina realized, trembling from head to toe. *Because he couldn't even put into words how much he needed her.*

Why hadn't she realized how much of his true self Kairos had revealed during sex? The power balance in their relationship—had it been more fluid than she'd thought?

She'd never really tried to understand him, never tried to look beneath the surface. She'd expected grand gestures and sweeping statements. And like a little girl denied what she wanted, she'd made his life hell for it.

But—thinking about it now—he had been twenty-seven when they had married, had been estranged from his adoptive family. He had had a rough upbringing, and neither of them had much experience with romantic relationships.

Had she taken any of that into account? Had she ever tried to reach him in a different way?

Non. All she had wanted was a fairy tale without putting any work into the relationship.

A long, filthy curse exploded from him, polluting the sunlit breakfast room. "*Dios*, Valentina! You should've told me if hurt you."

"You didn't. You never hurt me, Kairos. Whatever we did in bed, I was a willing, enthusiastic participant. So don't…don't make it a thing you did *to* me. Instead of with me. I craved the…" *the intimacy I found with you there* "…the pleasure you gave me. I told you that enough times."

His gaze darkened, a faint tension enveloping

his muscular frame. Things she didn't say swirled in that cozy glowing room.

He knew now how much she'd watched his every move, every gesture for meaning. How deprived she'd been for a single word of affection. Even a simple statement of his desire for her. For a word of praise—even if it was about those blasted pajamas she'd spent hours choosing. Or about her hair. Or her readiness for him whenever he wanted sex.

That he'd even liked her sexual appetite for him, was something she'd only realized when he'd cruelly commented on it on the yacht.

"You cannot doubt I found satisfaction with you." His gaze held hers in defiance and something else. As if only now he realized how much he had hurt her.

Legs shaking, she walked to the buffet table and poured herself another cup of coffee she didn't want. She took a sip just to force the lump in her throat down.

"I do not find relationships easy to manage."

Stunned that he would even make that concession now, she stared at him. If the consequences of that hadn't hurt her so much, she would have laughed at his mulish explanation.

"Those words would have meant a lot back then," she said sadly. "All I ever heard from you was criticisms."

"And every time I criticized you or compared you to Sophia or Alex, you fought back with an outrageous act," he said slowly, as if he was finally figuring it out.

"*Si.*" Her cup rattled loudly when she put it down on the table. "It's all in the past anyway."

If he had forced the discussion to continue, she'd have fled the room.

He went to the buffet. The clatter of cutlery behind her calmed her nerves.

Her relief was short-lived when he reached her, clasped her wrist in his rough fingers, tugged her and pushed her into the chair. The plate he deposited in front of her overflowed with fresh strawberries, a slice of toast and scrambled eggs.

Her stomach growled.

Without thanking him, Tina dug into it. Within minutes, she had polished off most of the breakfast.

She noticed only as she swallowed the last piece of the toast. Toast *he'd* prepared for her. Almost blackened, slathered in butter.

Just the way she preferred it.

Warmth bloomed in her chest. He'd noted that much about her. She tried to remind herself that it was too little. But the truth was there now that she wasn't in a fairy tale but real life.

Kairos had cared about her. It had been in all the little things he'd done for her. In the silences after they made love and the way he had held her as if she was precious, in the unsaid words between them after one of her escapades, in the way he had always encouraged her to come out from under her brothers' protective umbrella and make something of herself.

But how could she ever overcome the fact that she hadn't been enough? That she might never be good enough?

CHAPTER SIX

IT SEEMED IT was a day of shocks. No, a week of shocks.

From the moment he had set foot on the yacht and seen his wife dressed like a hooker to now, looking at the spreadsheet she showed him on her laptop screen.

Even the slide of her thigh against his couldn't distract his attention this time.

There were reams and reams of data in her pretty pink sketchbook and laptop.

While she pulled up different files—her lower lip caught anxiously between her teeth—he took a huge notebook and flipped it open.

Maybe two hundred pages were filled with sketches—dresses and accessories. Outfits put together from cutouts of dresses and hats and handbags. Pictures of people they had both known—Conti board members' wives and daughters and whatnot. And next to each person's photo cutout from some society pages were notes about how they were dressed wrong. Little corrections to their outfits, makeup, hair, shoes… Kairos idly flipped through the book, then picked up four more like the first one.

There were eight sketchbooks in all. It was years and years of work, he realized, shock vibrating through him.

"When did you start doing these?"

She shrugged, juxtaposing two different spreadsheets on her screen. "When I was eleven, twelve? About two years after I came to live with Leandro and Luca.

"I didn't really have a lot of clothes and accessories to play with until then. When they took me on that first shopping spree to this designer boutique…" Unadulterated joy filled her voice. She leaned back against the chair and closed her eyes, a smile playing at her lips. "It was like I was in heaven. I spent the whole day picking out dresses and shoes and hairbands and bows and belts and pins and more shoes… Leandro says I kept looking behind me every minute."

"Why?" Kairos asked automatically, even as he understood.

An uncomfortable tightness descended in his chest.

He'd forgotten that she hadn't always been this spoilt, rich Conti Heiress. It was the one time he'd wanted to go back for her after she'd walked out on him—when he'd heard the vicious rumor mill repeat the dirty truth.

Valentina Conti wasn't truly a Conti, but her mother's bastard with a chauffeur after she'd left the maniac Enzo Conti after years of abuse.

He had wondered who had leaked the news when the patriarch Antonio Conti and his grandsons Leandro and Luca Conti had hidden the truth for years; he wondered what it had cost Valentina to learn the truth.

A shimmer of doubt nagged at him.

"According to Luca, I was worried they would abandon me at the store and disappear. He says I was this little scrawny thing that would dig my nails in if he even loosened his grip around my hand." She straightened in her chair, her tone so devoid of emotion that the hair on the back of his neck prickled.

"Why?" he asked again.

He'd been married to her for nine months and he'd known nothing about her. *Christos*, he hadn't even been interested. He hadn't loved her, but he also knew firsthand what came of negligence. Of how simply holding back belief in someone could destroy one's belief in oneself.

Theseus had done that to him. And he had never recovered.

"I don't remember clearly actually. Even the bits I do, it's only because Luca would prod me softly. To make me remember. He said I would come running into his room or Leandro's in the middle of the night, crying and in panic. That for years, they would find me sleeping at the foot of his bed, one of my hands on his ankle.

"All I know is that there were months after my mom's accident before someone came looking for me. When Leandro found me and told me he was my older brother, he said I clung to him like a rabid dog."

When she seemed to be lost in the memories of the past, he tugged her hand into his. She returned the tight clasp before she opened her eyes and met his.

Such strength shimmered in her eyes that he felt singed by it. He could see why her brothers were so protective of her. Could see that little feral thing in her eyes. Could see the vulnerability that had always lurked beneath her dramatic personality.

Before he could say a word, she pulled her hand away.

"Valentina, who leaked the fact that you were not…a Conti?"

"I did," she replied instantly, her dark gaze holding his.

He sat back in his chair, reality as he knew it shifting and sliding. "Why?" It seemed to be the only word he could speak around her today. "How did you find out?"

"Sophia knew I was…miserable with you.

"Luca had told her about the circumstances of his birth, about how our mother left his father after his monstrous actions for years. About how Leandro sought to protect me from the truth. About why you married me.

"For the first time in my life, I had a friend who truly cared about me, who trusted me to have the courage to face the truth."

"What did she think it would solve?" He had always liked Sophia, but right now, he could happily wring her neck for interfering in his marriage.

"She thought the truth would free me from that

downward spiral I was in because you…" Again that shrug. "She was right. When I learned I wasn't a Conti, I realized how tightly I had clung to it because it had given me an identity when I'd been so scared and alone. When I learned about the alliance between you and Leandro…everything fell apart. If I wasn't Valentina Conti Constantinou, I was nothing. Something you told me again and again. It would only be a matter of time before you learnt the truth too, before you realized you hadn't gotten quite what you wanted. So I left."

Before you left me, the unspoken words reverberated between them.

That he measured so little in her estimation burned his gut. "I didn't leave you after Luca thwarted my fight to be the Conti CEO," he said, knowing it was the utter truth, "and I wouldn't have left you for not being the Conti heiress."

Instead of pacifying her, his words just caused a flash of that old temper to glitter in her eyes. "Do you even realize how arrogant that sounds? As if you were doing me a favor by keeping me on? I wasn't willing to find out what *would* drive you to leave me."

"Valentina—"

"Kairos, please don't pretend as if my leaving—once you get over your dented ego—didn't fill you with relief. It was a circus and it is done. Let it go."

It took every ounce of his self-control to let it go. Every inch of his pride to give in and admit failure. But her accusation that he was relieved… how dare she?

No, their marriage hadn't been great. Not even close to normal. They hadn't known each other at all.

But it was something he had begun to count on, even with her ridiculous, outrageous theatrics day after day.

She had become a constant in a life that had never known one.

The strength of the urge to punish her for disappointing him, for breaking her word to him, for thinking so little of him…the hurt driving that urge…it stunned him.

He fought the urge to swallow it away, to let it fester. If they were pulling skeletons out of the closet… "For what it's worth, I did hold our marriage sacred, Valentina. I counted on you sticking with me for the next fifty years or more. To have children with me, to build a family of our own… You showed me a glimpse of a future I'd never wanted before. And when it didn't work the way you wanted it to, you took it away, without even bothering to tell me. So don't you dare tell me what I felt when you walked away."

She had acted just as Theseus had once done. He had given Kairos everything and then snatched it away in the blink of an eye.

Maybe he should be glad that it was over with Valentina.

In nine months, he'd proved to himself—and her—that he didn't need her.

He wouldn't have seen her except for the divorce proceedings, if Theseus's situation hadn't forced him to seek her out.

And as she was so wisely reminding him, *she* had walked out. *She* had broken her promise. And that meant she wasn't worth all this thought, much less his regard.

His wife was what he had thought her initially—impulsive, immature and without loyalty.

"Let's just focus on the future like adults," he finally said.

Her throat stung as Kairos's words penetrated her defenses. For him to admit that her leaving had dented more than just his ego…

Her leaving had hurt him. So he had lashed out on the night at the yacht with cruel words. It didn't excuse it, but it explained so much.

She had been right. Kairos felt so much more than he ever let on.

What was she supposed to do with that knowledge? Why hadn't they ever talked like this before?

When she had talked about her childhood, she'd seen understanding.

Even a little flash of respect when she'd said *she'd* leaked that she wasn't a Conti. As if he hadn't thought her capable of shedding that safety blanket, that position of privilege. It was respect she craved with every cell in her body.

For a few minutes, he'd been kind. Understanding. Interested in her past and how it had shaped her. Interested in her—the person she was beneath the Conti tag—beyond what she could be for him.

But the admission about her leaving had cost him. The walls were back up, as if he had given her far too much.

Now, as she pointed to him several rows and columns, all she got was a polite stranger. The hard press of his thigh against hers, the graze of his corded forearm against the sides of her breasts as he pointed to the screen made her supremely aware of every inch of her body.

"What are all these names?" he asked pointing to the calls she'd highlighted.

"These are the names of the personnel I called at different couture houses—assistant buyers, vendors, designers' assistants and more."

He pulled the laptop to himself and browsed down. "There are almost...one hundred entries here. With times and dates."

She tried to shake off the vulnerability that descended on her. This was almost a year's worth of work. And she had nothing to show for it. For months, she would finish working a nine-hour workday, and then settle down to make calls. Humiliating chitchat, answering gossip about herself—she'd endured everything in the hope of getting the answer she wanted.

Nothing. Nada. Zilch.

"I kept a very thorough record."

"I see that. But what is it a record of?"

"Calls I made to different people over the last few months."

"You called all these people?" Disbelief rang in his tone, making her all prickly. When she tried to take the laptop from him, he resisted. "Answer me, Valentina."

"*Si.* I called all of them."

He ran a square-nailed finger against the column of Yes/No and the paltry maybes peppered through. "And what does this column mean?"

"It means whether they agreed to let me borrow the piece of clothing, the accessory or the shoes I called about. These are people who have access to the latest designer wear. Magazines and fashion houses and distributors and vendors, etc…"

"Why do you need all these? I thought you turned your back on things you couldn't afford? To attend parties with your pimp?"

That he still thought so little of her made her want to thump him. "I need a portfolio. As a stylist, whether a personal client or a house of design, it's the first thing clients and businesses want to see.

"I roped Nikolai into helping me do the photoshoot, and even enlisted an up-and-coming model to pose for me. But I don't have access to any clothes or shoes. Without that I have nothing."

"Weren't some of these people your friends? That one and that one…that guy?"

"*Si.*"

"But it says no against their names."

Tina gritted her teeth. "Are you being dense on purpose?"

One look at him told her he wasn't.

She sighed and rubbed her temple. "It's because they said no. They didn't say no to my face. Half of them wouldn't return my calls. And when I showed up at their workplace anyway, they had their minions tell me they were busy."

"Why?"

"I guess because word had spread that Leandro and Luca had abandoned me and that you dumped me after learning that I wasn't the esteemed Conti heiress. Only Nikolai would even talk to me. He got me that job. It took me a month to understand that none of my so-called friends were really friends. Just as you pointed out. Sophia, of course, offered the Rossi connections but I said no."

"That was foolish. The business world is nothing without connections and networking. You think I chose to ally myself with Leandro because I lacked business acumen? That I chose to head the CLG board because of the politics? Your brothers and Antonio have connections unlike anything I've ever known. I knew that if I wanted to go further in the business world, I needed more. I needed the powerful connections Leandro brought with him. I needed the old families to accept me into their circle."

It was the first time he had mentioned the agreement he had come to with Leandro. The agreement that had led to their marriage. It didn't sound as ruthless a transaction as she'd imagined.

"Are you giving me an explanation for why you did what you did? Perhaps asking for my forgiveness?" *Dios*, she was such a fool.

"No. The agreement we entered into is not that unusual. Leandro knew me. He knew that I would treat you well. And I—"

She glared at him. "But you didn't treat me well."

"Name one thing I deprived you of during our marriage."

"Respect. Affection. Regard." *Love.*

His silence was answer enough for Tina. "If I let Sophia help, then Luca would get involved, too. And if Luca got involved, Leandro would move heaven and earth to open every door for me. And soon, I would be drowning once again in my brothers' favors. I would forget why I started all this. I would become *that* Valentina."

He closed the laptop with a soft thud. With a glare, she hugged the thing to her chest. He took the laptop back from her clenched hands with exaggerated patience and set it down on the table. "Why *did* you start all this?"

She felt like an insect being examined under an industrial microscope. "I told you. I want to make something of myself."

His silver eyes pinned her to the spot. "What I'm asking is why you want to make something of yourself? What is this sudden need to prove yourself? Why all this hardship when before you couldn't even be bothered to understand anything beyond the little circle you were queen of?"

She couldn't tell him that he was the reason.

That she wanted his respect, his regard more than anything else in the world. That she wanted him to be proud of her. That she wanted him to regret—at length and at great pain—what he had lost by letting her go. Of course, she hadn't shed her vindictiveness.

"It's high time I took responsibility for myself. For my happiness, for my life," Tina repeated the lines she'd remembered Sophia spouting at her when she had been at her lowest.

All those things had significance, yes, but not in comparison to what she wanted to see in Kairos's eyes.

"So now that you have seen what I have done so far—" she opened her notepad and drew a couple of bullet points "—tell me the different ways you can help me. I know we talked about you putting word out to different friends of yours. But even if you succeeded in letting them hire me as their personal stylist, I would still need this portfolio to impress them, to gain their business. Now, with Nikolai and Marissa, I have a photographer and model lined up. All I need—"

"You're not working with that Russian joker anymore."

"You don't get to dictate who I talk to or not. You're not my husband anymore."

He pulled her left hand into his and awareness exploded through her. Callused fingers gripped hers, the pad of his thumb wiggling her wedding ring. "Officially, I am."

She pulled her hand away. "Nikolai's talented and he's proved that he has my best—"

"He wants to get in your pants, Valentina."

"I know he does. It doesn't mean he'll get there. Or that I want him there."

"You're not attracted to him."

The statement, which was really a question, arrested the millions of neurons firing away in her brain. Like complex machinery coming to a screeching halt.

Was that doubt in his question? A minute fracture in his arrogant confidence?

She wanted to lie and say she was attracted to Nikolai, to give him a taste of that uncertainty that had been her companion all during their marriage.

No games, Tina!

"I've never been interested in Nikolai. Not even before I met you." She cringed. "But I... I don't think I was kind in my rejection of him."

"What if he had attacked you that night on the yacht?"

The flippant response that rose to her lips arrested as Tina saw the whiteness of his knuckles. "I know him, Kairos. He's all bluster, and believe me, he has punished me enough with innuendoes and insults over the last few months. He's had his petty revenge. I have confidence that he'll be here when I ask him."

"I will not tolerate his sniffing around about you. You will entertain only me."

If her outrage could have been given action, Valentina would have had smoke coming out of her ears. She picked up her laptop and stood up. "I was a fool to think you'd take me seriously."

He gripped her arm and arrested her. "Even if I let you work with him, you still have no access to all the designer clothes and accessories you need. Unless you were thinking of asking me to buy them for you. As long as you—"

She covered his mouth with her palm. And instantly realized the foolishness of the move. His breath was warm against her palm, sending a rush of heat to her breasts and lower belly. As if he was touching his sensuous mouth to those places.

"*No*," she said and then cleared her throat. "I don't want you to buy anything for me. I only agreed to have my wardrobe back because my role as your loving wife demands it."

Was she never going to solve this Catch-22? What would she show prospective clients if she didn't have a portfolio to interest them, and how would she develop a portfolio if she never had clients?

Kairos pulled her hand away from his mouth but held it against his chest. His heart thundered against her fingertips. "You could join Theseus's company and try to achieve it that way. Go at your goal in a different way."

"Theseus's company?"

"He owns an advertising agency among the group. They put together a lot of shoots here and abroad to design the catalog for the luxury boutiques the Markos group holds all over Greece. A styling internship with such a company could get you valuable experience and contracts."

"And you can get me a position at his company just like that?"

"The woman who runs that department is a friend of mine. It'll be unpaid. Chiara's a no-nonsense go-getter who will only hold it against you that I got you the position."

"I'm willing to do any kind of work if it means I'm a step closer, Kairos. Being here with you when I'd rather mop floors at the fashion agency should prove that."

He ignored her petty barb. "But… Helena is in charge of that division. The moment she figures out you're there, she'll interfere."

"*No!*" Refusal escaped her lips even before she could process his words.

One thing she'd realized in the last week in his company was that she'd always be vulnerable when it came to Kairos. This proximity was bad enough without adding a woman who wanted him. A woman who shared history with him.

A woman who provoked every one of Valentina's baser, jealous instincts to the fore.

He tilted her chin up. "You do not have to be afraid of her, Valentina. She will not harm you, not while I'm here."

"That you have to reassure me of that speaks volumes."

"It's me she's after."

"I know that," she said, her voice going to that whiny octave she hated so much. That Helena wanted Kairos had been written in every malicious smile, every cruel remark of the past few days.

The whole situation twisted her gut. "I'll ask only this one question. Please, Kairos, answer it honestly."

He scowled, his fingers inching into the hair behind her ear tightly. The pad of his thumb pressed at her lower lip roughly. "I've never lied to you."

"Is this—" she waved her hand between them "—some elaborate ploy to make her jealous or to prove your power over her? To make her want you even more?"

At least, that was what Helena had hinted at over last night's dinner. That this thing between her and Kairos was a minor lovers' tiff. That he was using Valentina for any number of purposes.

"I have never played those kinds of games. With anyone."

No, those stupid games had been her forte. Observing Helena's antics was seeing a mirror version of her worst self.

"That doesn't answer my question."

"I don't want Helena."

"You never—"

"*Oxhi!* I wouldn't dishonor Theseus and Maria like that."

The depth of relief that spread in her chest scared the hell out of Tina. This was so not the time to discover Kairos's honorable streak or any other fine qualities. *Dio mio*, he was not for her. "But Theseus and Maria…they want you for their daughter. They think of you as their son. It was clear they—"

"Thinking of me as their son and being their son is different, Valentina. In the end, blood wins." His nostrils flared, the topic clearly hitting a nerve. "At least, that's been my experience."

Because Theseus had chosen Helena to head the company over him the last time? Tina had gathered that much from the hints Helena had dropped over the last few days. And from the obvious tension between Theseus and Kairos every time the discussion shifted to the companies.

She pushed out of his hold, needing to think clearly. "I can't work with Helena."

"Opportunities like this internship won't come your way often."

"I'll somehow—"

"You won't. If it's not this job, it will be a troublesome client. If not Helena, someone else to whom you would have to grovel. The fashion industry, whether here or in Milan, is cutthroat. Full of pitfalls and backstabbing men and women. There's no shame in knowing your shortcomings. No shame in giving up."

Tina stared at him. "Giving up?"

"Aren't you? You'll be here for at least three

months, and you're turning down a position in the field you want to work in. Not that I'm surprised."

"Your pride—which is a monumental thing—got bruised because I left you. And for that, you're punishing me by making me work for her."

His mouth twitched. "Actually, I have always thought you and Helena were cast from the same mold. All glitter and no substance."

She'd thought the same, yet the laughingly delivered comment punched Tina hard. Her chest tightened. Did he think so little of her? Still?

All glitter and no substance.

No words could encompass her so well. No one had ever stripped all pretense, all her armor, and laid her bare like that.

This intimacy, his admission that their marriage had been sacred to him, it was making her forget what kind of a man he was. Making her forget that there was no place in his life for anything but ambition.

"You know, from the moment you told me you 'needed' your wife, I've been wondering why." She stilled at the wide doors to the courtyard, the sun caressing her bare arms. The villa, the grounds, everything was paradise. Sharing a room with the man she'd given her body and soul to, pretending that they adored each other, was incredibly seductive.

A thin line of tension appeared between his brows. "I told you why."

"But not all of it."

Silence stretched. She waited, wanting him to offer to tell her. Wanting him to want her to know the truth about his present, his past. About the ruthless choices that seemed to define his life.

To want to make her understand him.

"And what did you figure out?" Pure steel in his voice.

"Maria said that you flew to Theseus's side the moment you heard of his heart attack. That you held off a hostile takeover on his board that would've wrenched control from Theseus. And Helena mentioned that you had almost been engaged. She clearly adores you still. But there's tension between all of you. It's clear that you had a falling out, something that prevented you and Helena from being together the last time around. You saved his life and his company…"

A brow rose on his face, his hip cocked out at a jaunty angle, but still he waited. Ruthlessness dripped from his very pores. "Make your point, *pethi mou.*"

"I think you saw an opportunity."

Any hint of charm disappeared from his eyes. "What opportunity would that be, Valentina?"

Even as he asked the question, there was a warning in his words.

Not to voice it. Not to give form to her thoughts. But she wanted to fracture that icy control, that smooth, uncaring facade. Bloodthirsty by nature, she wanted him to tell her the whole truth. To admit that her accusations hurt.

"You want to take over Theseus's company but not his daughter, so you produced me to pretend we have a perfect marriage. I haven't quite figured out why you can't get rid of me and marry her, and then you would have everything you want. But what I know is that when you have the company in hand, you'll discard me, leash Helena and become the CEO. What else would motivate you to put your life on hold except the fact that you can gain power by this move?"

A cold smile sliced his cruel mouth upwards. "And here I worried that Helena would twist your mind with lies."

There was such a wealth of emotion in his tone

that Tina's heart pounded. "Will you deny that at the end of all this you'll own Theseus's company?"

"No."

"That you brought me here to deceive that sweet couple, to avoid Helena's attentions?"

"No."

"Then where is the lie in what I said, Kairos?" She waited for him to deny her accusation, to give her another reason. Anything for her to hold onto, a chance for them.

"Everything you do, every decision you make, it's to acquire more wealth. More power. More connections." She thought she was over the worst but it only hurt to see the coldness in his eyes. "Why should this be any different, when all that ever motivates you is ambition?"

CHAPTER SEVEN

EVERYTHING YOU DO is motivated by ambition.

Valentina's words played like a broken record through his mind even after a month. Taking another sip of his throat-burning Scotch, Kairos admitted it grated still.

For years after he had walked away from Theseus, all he had been able to think of was how to advance, how to prove to Theseus—and himself—that he could make it work without his former mentor's help. And without Theseus's legacy.

In that blind drive, he had developed a reputation for ruthless deals and an expertise in getting rid of broken parts of a company. He had forgotten that there was more to life than business deals and the next takeover. A fact Leandro had pointed out when he had first met him.

He smiled. The man was a master strategist if ever there was one. But his words had sunk in. And once he had seen Valentina, he had wanted her. The idea of marriage, settling down, making a family of his own…had held appeal.

He'd seen it as another forward move in his life, not an adjustment.

Or maybe his mistake had been to let his libido choose the wrong wife. Maybe if he hadn't been so obsessed with winning Valentina, hadn't reveled in how artlessly she had fallen for him, he would have said no to Leandro's offer.

Leaning back into his seat, he swept his gaze around the nightclub. His tension deflated a little when he found Helena dancing with one of the younger board members on Markos's board of directors.

Valentina's accusation had been correct…and yet also not correct at the same time. It rankled that she thought so little of him, that he would take advantage of Theseus in his feeble state. And yet he had balked at explaining himself.

The more she delved beneath his surface, the more he wanted to hide himself away.

Why did it feel like giving Valentina a piece of the past was giving her a part of his soul? Why didn't the damn woman revert to what he had considered her default?

Restlessness slithered in his blood. Even the

brutal three-hour-a-day training he had been pushing on his body, in preparation for a triathlon, was still not enough to rid his body of that simmering energy.

And his sweet, little wife was the cause.

It was close to a month now since she had accepted that position in the ad agency. A month of waiting to receive a call from Chiara that Valentina had slapped someone, or fought with someone, or that she had stormed out because she had had to work too hard.

Not a peep from his wife's boss or Helena or Valentina about her job. Not a single complaint.

They had sort of fallen into a routine as husband and wife far too easily—they had started running together in the morning, breakfasting together, and then he gave her a lift to work and they parted ways. Most evenings, they dined with Theseus and Maria until either he or she went back to work again.

And then came the long torturous nights.

His balls, he was afraid, were permanently going to shrivel if he had to take one more cold shower, if he had to untangle Valentina from himself in the middle of one more night.

She thought him a ruthless bastard anyway. So

what stopped him from taking what he wanted like he'd always done?

If he waited on some twisted notion of honor, he'd have had nothing in life. He'd have still been foraging through some dumpster in the back alleys of Athens, ended up either dead or pimping some poor prostitute to make a life. It was only by taking what he wanted he'd gotten this far in life.

He wanted sex—*Christos*, it was all he could think of—and he had a wife who matched him in his fervor for sex if nothing else. So what the hell was he feeling guilty about?

She was changing how he saw her, and she was changing him from the inside out.

Why else did his gut clench when he saw the shadows under her eyes, when he saw her weave tiredly through dinner? Why else did he want that adoration, that love back in her eyes?

Was celibacy making him sentimental?

Andaxi!

He ordered another glass of Scotch—his second, which was one more than he ever allowed himself, when he heard the soft hush around his table. The hairs on the back of his neck prickled.

Desire came at him in that same visceral punch

when his gaze found her. But with that ever-present hum came a bubble of laughter bursting out of his throat. The shocked silence around the table was enough proof that he rarely laughed like that.

He should have known she would do something like that. Knew the subdued shadow she was making herself into was...unnatural for her.

Thrown into brilliance by the multicolored strobe lights from the bar, her copper-colored sheath dress with a million metallic chips contrasted dazzlingly against her golden skin tone. The material clung to her chest and waist like a lover's hands and then ended just below the thin flare of her hips.

His mouth dried. Her gaze swept through the club, landed on him.

The long, toned muscles of her thighs when she moved...it was pure sensuality in motion. Five-inch stiletto heels made her legs go on for miles. Her hair was in its usual braid.

Only he knew how the silky mass would caress a man's face or how it provided an anchor to hold on to when he was driving into her wet heat. She wore no jewelry except those plain diamond studs at her ears that were a gift from Luca, and the pendant he'd given her. A foolish piece of sentimentality he'd indulged in.

His knuckles gripped the seat as she reached their table and every man's gaze in the vicinity devoured her.

A subtle thread of her fragrance wafted over him as she bent and kissed his cheek.

"Hello, Kairos," she said, wrapping her arms around him from behind. Her breasts pressed against his neck. Sensations assaulted him, his muscles curling with the control it took not to clamp his mouth over hers.

Slowly, that initial roar of desire settled into a simmering hum. Clarity came.

For a month, she'd been so careful around him. Never touching him unless necessary and unless they had an audience. Even then, he could feel the tension in her frame every time he came near her. Could feel her flinch every time he touched her.

Now, she was all over him. And instead of leading her into one of the backrooms specifically reserved for couples who wanted private space and taking her against the wall as every instinct was riding him to, he found himself frowning.

One elbow over the back of his seat, she looked

down at him. Shadows swirled in her eyes, hiding what he wanted to see.

"Are you drunk?"

"I had three glasses of white wine while I dressed in Chiara's personal suite after your high command."

He noted the jut of her collarbone, the bluish shadows under her eyes. "Did you remember to eat before the wine?"

She scrunched her forehead. "No wonder it went straight to my head. You'll have to put it down to the shock that you ordered me to meet you in a nightclub, of all places. That's like—" she frowned, her lower lip jutting out "—the old me going to a sale in a department store, or being kind to Claudia Vanderbilt. Or the new me succeeding at something." She laughed.

Beneath the low, husky sound, Kairos found something disconcerting. A hint of pain.

It wasn't just the dress. Her lips were painted a dark voluptuous red—the only feature she possessed that was plump and lush. It was a color he'd once forbidden her to wear.

Because, throughout the formal dinner with his new business partners one night, all he'd been able to think of was kissing that mouth, of wanting his innocent wife's lush mouth wrapped around his cock even as she goaded his temper by flirting outrageously with another man across the table.

Something was wrong. Because whenever something went wrong in his wife's little world, she acted like a teenage rebel.

It had taken him this long to understand the pattern. For a smart man, he lost all capability for logic and rationality when it was Valentina.

She'd slapped Sophia when he'd refused to define his relationship with her.

She'd stripped and jumped into a pool in her underwear at a venture capitalist's retreat in Napa Valley because he'd told her in no uncertain terms that they weren't there for fun but business. A fact she'd been made aware of well in advance.

When he'd forced her to return the Bugatti she'd had delivered for his birthday present—bought with her brother's money no less—she'd decided to return it recklessly and almost hit a tree in her anger.

All actions that had infuriated him.

Was this another ploy?

But what he saw this time was vulnerability in her gaze. The tremble in her fingers as she picked up his drink and took a sip. The fine lines of tension around her forehead.

Valentina never indulged in spirits at least. Something to do with her mother's accident. And yet, here she was, not completely sloshed but without the wariness and inhibition he'd spied in her eyes in the last month.

The booth was U-shaped and he was sitting at the end. "Let me see the back of your dress," he taunted, some devil in himself goading him.

She turned around obligingly, moving with an innate grace that had captured his attention the first time he'd met her. He gritted his teeth. He was right.

The fabric barely covered her buttocks. But *Christos*, his palms ached to cup them, to pull her flush against him until she felt what she did to him.

"You asked me to join you at a nightclub." Her gaze swept over the club and landed on Helena leaning against the bar and watching them with a smirk. The glitter in his wife's eyes brightened as her gaze swept over the cool blue knee-length dress Helena wore. In contrast to Valentina, he noticed now, she looked elegant, refined.

His wife's tension doubled. "I assumed it was to put on a show for Helena."

He pulled her down to sit beside him. "How has she been treating you?"

"Nothing I can't handle. Except the little snippets of your history that she keeps dropping around the team. How many favors Theseus did you. How many disappointments you've had to face in life. I think everyone on the team realized she was talking about me."

"Valentina—"

"She doesn't bother me, Kairos."

"No?"

She shrugged. "All the scenarios she desperately tries to plant in my head would have driven me crazy if...you still meant something to me." She looked up then and smiled. But the smile didn't touch her eyes. "Anyway, I came armed with the weapons I possess."

"Weapons?" he said, his mouth twitching. For all he tried, he couldn't muster disappointment or anger that she'd shown up dressed like a...delectable morsel he wanted to consume.

He felt anticipation and tenderness. For something was definitely not right and he wanted to fix it for her.

"She flaunts her breasts in your face every opportunity she gets. I don't have big breasts or flaring hips. My legs are my weapons and I decided to showcase those."

He rubbed his fingers over his face, fighting the urge, but laughed out loud anyway. He had a feeling it would hurt her feelings. And it had, if the way she gripped the table showing white knuckles was anything to go by.

"Twisted, *si*? That my insecurity about my body has finally found your sense of humor?"

Just like that, his smile disappeared. "What in God's name are you talking about now?"

"The fact that I obsessed for nine months over your fascination with my lack of melons."

"Melons?" he said, almost choking on the sip of his whiskey.

She mock-cupped her hands in front of her chest like men did when they talked about big breasts. "You know…jugs. Bazookas."

His mind roiled, came to a jarring conclusion. "*Christos*, is that why you took to wearing those obscenely ridiculous push-up bras? Because you assumed I was into big breasts?"

Color streaked along her cheekbones. "*Si*. I wanted to please you. I was naive and foolish enough to believe that the illusion of big breasts would somehow make you appreciate me more. Make your nonexistent heart beat."

"I hated those bras. When I touched you…all I could feel was padding." He muttered another oath. "Where in hell would you get the idea that I liked big breasts?"

"From things you said when we watched old Hollywood movies. From the way all your love interests were built in the front. From the way you never…" She looked away, her throat bobbing up and down.

He turned her to his side until she faced him. Strips of light caressed the high sweep of her cheekbones. The narrow blade of her nose. She licked her lips nervously. He couldn't be distracted. At least not yet.

"I never what, Valentina?"

She shuffled her legs under the table but he wouldn't let her budge. In the end, she ended up piling her legs above and around his. It was the closest he'd been to her in months. Fever took root in his muscles.

"I don't know why we're talking about this."

"Because I want to know."

"Francesca Pellegrini told me that her husband was obsessed with her breasts." Her cheeks burned. "But when we made lo—when we had sex, you never...spent a lot of time with my breasts. So I assumed you didn't like them. There? Are you happy? Or would you like more humiliating details from our marriage?"

"Did it not occur to you that I might have just been in a hurry to get to other places? That unlike Francesca Pellegrini's husband—who by the way always gawks at you, the old pervert—I might be a leg man?" he whispered, not knowing whether to laugh or groan.

She had built up so many things in her head and it was his fault. He had incessantly found fault with her.

Shame settled in his chest. He ran his knuckles over the lean line of her leg, and her breath hitched.

"You have legs that go on for miles, *glykia mou*. You're so tall that I don't get a crick in my neck when I kiss you. You fit so perfectly against me that I could hold you against the wall and be inside you in a second. When I'm inside you and you wrap your legs around me..." He cleared his throat, forgetting where he was going for a second. "But of course, forgive me for my oversight." He let his gaze rove over the deep V plunge of her neckline. His blood became sluggish, his erection an insistent ache in his trousers. "I promise to spend more time with your breasts in the near future."

A choking gasp fell from her mouth. Her eyes sparked outrage. "You're not getting anywhere near my breasts."

He raised a brow, loving the warm flush on her cheeks. "We'll see about that."

A waiter brought some appetizers he had ordered. He picked up a piece of cheese and held it to her mouth. "Eat."

She shook her head, held his gaze defiantly and took another sip of his Scotch.

"You're acting like a child. You'll be sick if you chase wine with Scotch. You don't do well with alcohol."

She pouted, leaning back against the seat. "You don't like dancing, you don't want me to drink and you don't like for me to have any fun. Why am I here then? If it's for Helena's sake, you should know she doesn't buy our reunion."

"Let Helena think whatever she pleases."

"Please, Kairos. The truth, for once. Why are you here?"

"When one of the board members suggested we check out the new club, I joined them. Georgio," he said nodding at the man standing close to Helena, his angelic features visible even from here, "is—"

"Alexio Kanapalis's son," she said, shocking him into stupefied silence. "Alexio tried to get the vote to oust Theseus from his own board. You booted him out instead. But Georgio stayed. So you wonder if Georgio's loyalty lies with his father or with Theseus. Of course, that he's so... chummy with Helena goes in its own column of uneasy matters."

He stared at her.

She laughed. "I'm not stupid. Georgio visits my department all the time. All the ladies swarm around the pretty boy cooing over his perfectly symmetric features and all that dark blond hair. Not counting his charm and wit, he reminds me a bit of Luca."

"Stay away from him, Valentina."

She sighed. "How many men will you order me to stay away from?"

He ignored her question, but didn't quite succeed at ignoring the jealousy in his gut, however, when Tina looked at the other man and his damned perfect features. "In nine months of living together, you never once had an inkling of my business affairs."

She scrunched her nose at him. "Because I didn't care. Not because I didn't lack intellect."

"And now you're interested?"

"*Si.*"

"Why?"

"Because as soon as you figure out who's behind all this, Theseus and you will come to an agreement, and the sooner I'll be out of your life. Forever this time."

Her eagerness to be done with their charade made him grit his teeth. "It wasn't just to keep an eye on Georgio and Helena," he admitted. She was always so damned honest with him. Was he such a coward that he couldn't even admit small things to her? "You've been working far too hard. I thought you would like to have a change of pace for one night."

"Did Theseus comment that you've not shown me any sights? Has Helena poked a hole in our happily-ever-after?"

The brittleness in her smile tugged at him.

"Does there have to be a reason to want to see my wife?"

"Ah…you want sex. What did you assume— you'd spend two hours being nice to me and I'd let you screw me in the back room? I'm sure there are any number of women, including Helena, who'll be happy to be your screw toys."

He gripped her chin in his hand, anger and hurt riding him hard. *Christos*, only Valentina could turn him into a little boy. "Your insults to my character are getting annoying, Valentina. Is it so hard to believe that I wanted to give you a night away from the villa? From work?"

"*Si*, it is. You don't do anything without a motive or a goal, Kairos."

Yes, he meant to keep an eye on Helena and Georgio, but he'd wanted to give Valentina a night out on the town, too.

But his wife was as receptive as a porcupine.

Whose fault is that? Have you ever treated her as a partner, as an equal?

He slid the small package he'd had delivered the minute he'd finished his call with her brother, and pointedly ignored the awkward silence that fell when she saw it.

Leaning toward her, he kissed her cheek. Her shoulders tensed, a sudden stillness enveloping her.

God, she had such silky soft skin. All over.

His favorites were the incredible sensitive skin of her inner thighs, the neatly delineated curve where her tiny waist flared into hips, and the skin right below her right buttock where she had another mole.

He remembered her body like it was a map to some treasure.

"Happy birthday, Valentina."

She went still. "Who reminded you?"

When he didn't answer, she turned to him. "I know you're not big on remembering or celebrating birthdays and anniversaries."

His laughter when she'd joyously given him the platinum cuff links for one month of their marriage reverberated between them. He'd thought it hilarious that she bought expensive gifts for him with her brother's money without batting an eyelid.

She'd pouted prettily, argued that he was laughing at a romantic gesture.

He remembered the crushed look in her eyes

when he'd blithely stated that it had probably cost her nothing to charge her brother's card.

Dios, he'd been an uncaring jerk of the first order. If she'd been juvenile and volatile, he'd been cruel and ruthless.

When he'd realized the wife he had acquired as part of a merger was not the elegant, refined socialite he could be proud of, not the political asset he could count on, but a living, breathing creature with feelings and wishes, he'd resented her.

When she'd avowed love for him, he'd pitied her for her grand delusions. Become indifferent to her, waited for her to grow out of it.

When she'd started acting out, he'd been infuriated.

Not once had he realized how much vulnerability she had hidden beneath the fiery temper and impertinence. How honest she'd always been.

He wouldn't have fallen in love with her, but he could have been kinder to her. He was a man who thrived and succeeded in actively hostile environments—he could have molded her to what he wanted in a wife with one kind word or a romantic gesture.

Yet, he'd rigidly shut her out. As a clever business man, his own actions didn't make sense to him. He had used her for only one thing. And he'd made up his mind to do it again before discarding her for good.

Her slender fingers fiddled with the strings on the small package. "Kairos?"

He cleared his throat. "Leandro called me last night. He said it was the first birthday in years that you were spending away from them. He asked where you were and what I had dragged you into."

She pushed the gift away from her with such force that the small package flew off the other end of the table. She pinned him with a furious gaze. "I told him to stay out of my life." Her chest fell and rose with her harsh breaths. "I told you our deal was off if you even spoke to one of them behind my back."

When he'd have calmly walked away before, he said, "I told him this was between you and me."

He tugged her wrist when she'd have walked away. "They're simply worried about you. About what you're doing back with me. About your job and even about your safety—"

"Because no one thinks I can take care of myself. That I'm capable of being anything other than a naive sister or a trophy wife. No, wait, you've made it clear that I failed at even that. Not much of a trophy, am I?"

Somehow, she loosened his grip on her and walked away. She cut a wide swathe through the crowd, her hips swaying.

It was only one of her tantrums, he told himself.

He was not going to chase her like some love-sick boyfriend.

She had lasted a month—a miracle in itself—before that cloak of serenity had been ripped. Just what he had expected.

There had been innumerable occasions when she'd lost it just like that. And Kairos had always let her stew in it. He'd always set the boundaries so she would understand that he would never indulge her juvenile temper.

She would come back to him. She always had done. She would walk back in, and he'd pretend like nothing was wrong.

Until one day, she had left. Walked out, a voice mocked.

Until now, he'd attributed it to her foolish, romantic delusions but for the first time, he had to consider the possibility that he had driven her away. That he hadn't been the man she needed.

Punishing Valentina for walking out on him, seducing her and then discarding her...the very idea felt wrong now. Without honor. Yet what was the alternative?

Running his hands through his hair, he cursed long and hard.

Did he want to keep her? Knowing now that she'd always want something he couldn't give. Something he didn't know how to do.

And even if he did, his blind confidence all these days that Valentina would come back to him smacked of arrogance.

All he knew was that he was far from done with her. And she... *Christos*, even without trying this past month, the woman still had her hooks in him. There was passion between them and if he allowed it, there could be respect and even affection maybe.

Was there a chance for them?

Right now, all he knew was that she was hurt, that she needed a friend. And for once, he wanted to be everything Valentina needed.

CHAPTER EIGHT

Tina knew she was acting childishly, just as Kairos had predicted. She knew she was letting her emotions rule her head once again.

But she couldn't just sit there, with the pity gift he'd probably had his assistant order for her, mocking her. God, she hated herself for the leap in her pulse when he'd kissed her cheek, the hope bubbling in her throat when he'd placed the present in front of her.

She couldn't face him knowing that sooner or later he was going to find out what a spectacular failure she was; couldn't pretend anymore that being around him—seeing him day in and day out—wasn't wearing her down.

She walked away from the dance floor into the interior of the nightclub.

Black marble gleamed at her feet. Slowly, the music and noise from the crowd faded. She reached a door marked VIP lounge and hesitated.

When the six-foot-tall guard let her through without raising a brow, she slipped into the room.

The silence in the room was absolute. It was properly soundproofed. Black leather sectionals lined the entire back wall. Except for soft recessed lighting, the room was all shadows. She opened the refrigerator built discreetly into the wall. More wine and champagne.

It was so tempting to have some more. To bury the sensation of sinking, the bitterness of knowing that Kairos was right about her.

Instead she took out a bottle of water. She picked up one of the remotes. The music system, built into the walls, came on. Alicia Keyes crooned out a love song.

Sighing, she turned to the wall that was completely glass and looked down to the dance floor.

She sensed Kairos's presence behind her even before she heard him. Her spine felt like it would crack in two at the rigidness she infused into it. For a man who was six foot four and built like a bouncer, he'd always moved with such economy of movement. She chanced a quick look.

He was leaning against the door. Black dress shirt and black trousers—he could have blended into the shadows if didn't have such an electric presence. Goose bumps rose over her arms, remembered sensations zigzagging over her skin.

It had been foolish to think he wouldn't follow her. Right now, she was sort of an important asset to his complex machinery. Why had she trapped herself in here with him? Especially in the reckless mood she was in.

Even though they had shared a bedroom for the last month, she had left herself no chance to be alone with him. He worked late most nights, closeted in the study with Theseus and after sixteen-hour days with barely a break for dinner, she had been falling into exhausted sleep.

Now they were enclosed in the dark room—every sound and sight of the outside world cut off, electricity charging the air. His desire was like a scent she couldn't escape and every cell in her responded to it.

He'd never given her anything as a husband—not a word of praise, not a token gift, not a gesture of affection. But the knowledge of his desire for her, and that it seemed unquenchable, was a powerful aphrodisiac. It filled her with a false feeling of power over him, over this situation between them.

She turned and faced him, the harsh beauty of

his face stealing her breath away. "Go back to your…strategies. Christian will drive me back to the house."

He prowled into the dark room, picked up the bottle she had left on the table and emptied it within seconds. "You're upset. You've been upset from the minute you walked into the nightclub. What happened?"

His concern, shockingly, was genuine. And it would only make her weak. "I won't run away in the middle of the night, if that's what you are worried about."

His growl was soft yet so loud in the sound-proofed room. Goose bumps broke out on her skin. "Forget about the damned company for a second, Valentina. Forget about Theseus and Maria and Helena. Forget about our godforsaken pretense of a marriage. I'm asking you to tell me what's bothering you. Whatever it is, I will solve it for you."

"I don't want your help or your damn pity gift, or your concern."

"It is not a pity gift. I feel any number of things for you, Valentina, but pity is not one of them."

"I don't want any more clothes or jewelry or shoes. Giving me those things when I insist that they don't matter to me anymore only hurts me. Deeply." She hugged her middle. "I never thought you were a particularly cruel man. Heartless, but not cruel."

"It is not any of those things." His breath hissed out. "And I don't... I don't like hurting you. I never wanted to. Well, except for that night when I found you on the yacht."

"What is it then? The gift?"

"A subscription to an American network channel that streams Westerns. All you have to do is plug in the serial number on that card and you can stream an unlimited number of shows and movies." His mouth pursed at her silence. "I heard you and Theseus discuss them the other day. It would be a good way to pass Saturdays. He loves it when you join him to watch those movies."

Shock enveloped her, followed by a rush of such powerful joy that she felt dizzy. "I...don't know what to say." She felt vulnerable, small. The strength of what she felt for him...she shook from it.

A flash of light illuminated his face. His nostrils flared, his mouth tightened. "I was cruel and harsh toward you that night. All through our marriage, really. I don't know diplomacy with you. I don't know how to soften my words. You…you weren't what I expected. Your days were filled with shopping and parties. You dressed outrageously. You flirted with every man you met—"

"I only did that after we were married," she shouted into the dark.

"How is that better?" He spoke more and more softly, gritting the words out.

With every step he took toward her, she stepped back. "I flirted to make you jealous. I flirted to get your attention. I flirted with friends who knew why I was doing it and who pitied my pathetic efforts. Because I was married to an uncaring beast."

He stilled. And if she weren't so miserable, Valentina could have laughed at the absurdity of it all. Hadn't he realized such a small thing?

"I didn't succeed even then, did I? You had no regard for me, I knew—"

He continued as if she hadn't interrupted him. But any hint of warmth she'd seen earlier was gone. His eyes were chips of the coldest frost. His jaw set into a granite cast.

"You drove me crazy, Valentina. I couldn't concentrate in meetings for worry of which party you would show up at that night, or with whom you would flirt all evening, or what hijinks you would get up to because I refused to cut the single friend I had. I canceled my trips abroad because I was worried what scandal you'd get into behind my back. I couldn't sleep when I went to Beijing because I was so worried you'd stay out too long with those useless friends of yours in some damn club with no one to look after you. I wanted a wife—instead you were like a child, who wanted the latest, shiniest, most expensive toy.

"I didn't know when you would decide you'd had enough of me. When you would ask your bloody brothers to purchase you a new man. When you would decide that you didn't want me in your bed anymore. When you would decide to welcome another man into your body—"

Her hand flew at his cheek. The sound reverberated in the silence like the crack of thunder.

Valentina gasped, waves of pain radiating up her arm. Still, that pain was nothing compared to the hurt in her chest. His head jerked back but he didn't even touch his cheek.

Her chest heaved, her breath rattling against the outrage she felt. "I've never looked at, much less thought of, another man since the first evening I saw you. Yes, I was shallow, naive, I had no purpose in my life. But what I gave to you, I gave it with conviction, with loyalty. You wanted a robot you could screw at night, a trophy you could display to the world during the day. You don't know how to give, Kairos. But you don't know how to receive, either. That first month… God, I was deliriously happy because of the orgasms you doled out. You shouldn't have married me when you don't know how to have a simple relationship."

She made to get away from him but his arm snagged around her waist. She fell into his side, her breasts and belly pressed up against his hard body. Her breath was punched out of her, shallow and serrated. One hard thigh tangled between hers, rubbing at the center of all the ache. Wetness pooled at her sex, soaking into her flimsy thong.

A whimper fell from her mouth as she tried to move back and rubbed up a little more against him. One arm stayed tight around her waist while he lifted her chin with the other.

His silvery eyes glowed with unbanked desire. Both his hands gripped her hips now. Such large hands that his fingers could always easily span her waist. Her breath fell in soft pants, which seemed amplified in the room.

"It's been more than ten months, now, Valentina. I've been going crazy with wanting you."

Her eyes widened. "I don't believe you. You…"

"Because I'm so dishonorable that I would bed another woman while my wife is missing? Because one woman is the same as the next for an ambitious, ruthless man like me? Because I didn't miss you in bed with a longing that eats at me, a hunger that I can't control?"

"Then why didn't you come after me?"

"Because I don't need you, Valentina."

He growled the words out loud as if he could make them true and yet Tina knew that he meant them. Everything seemed to tilt and shift, the flash of hurt in his eyes when she'd called him a robot, not imagined but real.

For the first time, he felt like a flesh-and-blood man. He was determined to prove to her, and more important, to himself, that he didn't need her.

Why was he so determined to keep her out, to pretend that he didn't care? The gift, this night, his care for her when she was exhausted—everything said he did care.

Further thought was extinguished when his mouth fell onto hers with a rapacious hunger. Relief poured through her, twisting with need. She missed his body, the sense of excitement and danger as he toppled her inhibitions one by one. She missed his bruising kisses, his insatiable appetite that drew out her pleasure until she was begging him, even the epithets that flew from his lips during sex.

His tongue plunged into her mouth, sliding and stroking around her own. Power. Passion. Possession. His mouth stamped all of them over hers. His stubble rasped roughly against her jaw, her lips stinging from the torturous pleasure.

Her hands roamed all over him—the broad shoulders, the muscled arms, the defined chest. The thud of his heart filled her with a reckless urgency. Just tonight, she promised herself. Just a few kisses.

His hands sunk into her hair, pulling at it roughly as he tilted her face up. Rough and hard, he kissed her as if he meant to devour her. As if she had finally pushed him over the edge.

She reveled in the pain and the pleasure his grip forced on her. Moans and whimpers, the sounds she made filled the quiet room. Her eyelids fell, her breath was not her own. An explosion of color filled her body as his mouth left hers to trail down her jaw. Featherlight kisses alternated with hard, guttural words from him in Greek.

She tugged at his hair, desperate to be closer. She shuddered as he sank his teeth into the crook of her neck. Her pulse beat fervently against his tongue. He closed his mouth against the tender skin and sucked. Tremors raced across her skin, pooling between her legs. He swept his tongue over the tender hurt. "Look at me, *pethi mou*. Look at what you drive me to, still. Look at what you turn me into."

Raw desire glittered in his eyes. Tina gasped as cold glass pressed against her bare buttocks. And in front of her he was a cauldron of desire. Heat blasted up her neck and into her cheeks as she realized he had walked her to the back of the room. Shock and desire made her voice strange, husky. Fingers bunching into his shirt, she fought the sensual haze. "We're…they can…"

"No one can see you but me, Valentina. No one knows this body except me, *ne*? Let them be witness to what you drive me to. Let me take you here, in a public place with nothing but a flimsy piece of glass separating us from the crowd. Does this tell you how much control I have? Does that tell you what insanity you drive me to?"

His hands tugged her dress up. Madness filled her body. Rough hands pulled her leg up to wrap it around his hip. She moaned loudly. Her aching sex pressed into his pelvis like that. So close. So hard. Head thrown back into the glass, Tina let herself drown in the sensation.

Nothing else remained anyway. Nothing she was good for. She wanted to gorge on the sensations he created. One callused hand cupped her buttock while one hand roughly pushed her thong out of the way. Gaze holding hers, he simply covered her mound with his palm. All the roughness, all the urgency faded. Soft and exploring, his fingers stroked the lips of her sex.

The intimacy of it in such a public place pushed her arousal to the edge. Her heart pounded, she was past rationality.

Slowly, his fingers separated her folds and dipped inside.

"You're wet. So ready for me. Always ready for me."

It was a statement that rang with masculine pride. Her palms flat against the glass, she shivered as he spread the dampness around her opening in mind-numbing circles with a thoroughness that cinched her body into a tight knot.

"Please, Kairos," she whispered, burying her mouth in his neck. Roughly, she dragged the lapels of his shirt apart, until a button popped. She was ravenous for him. For his skin, For his taste. She licked the strong column of his throat. Tasted the sweat and masculinity of him.

He growled, the sound bursting out of his chest. His hand left her buttock. Valentina moaned in protest. But he only laughed. With deft movements, he undid the knot at the back of her neck.

The silky strings fell over her chest. His silver gaze held hers, a wicked smile curving his sensuous mouth. Slowly, he pulled the strings down.

Down, down, down until the dress flopped at her waist. It bunched around her hips, leaving her breasts and her sex exposed to his devouring gaze.

He looked like a marauder from the dark ages, the stamp of desire on his hard features. His gaze moved to her breasts. They were brown tipped and tight from the cold air kissing their pert tips. His breath fell in hot strokes. Their gazes held. Breath was fire in her throat. Callused fingers cupped their meager weight. Molded and cupped. He drew maddening circles around the aching tips.

And he bent, licking one engorged tip. Again and again. This breast and then that breast. He cupped them and pushed them up, his tongue flicking around and around. "You were right. I was a selfish bastard to have ignored these. To have overlooked what pleasure I could bring you by touching you here. Never again, *pethi mou*. Never will I neglect these again." And then, as if to seal his promise, he opened his mouth and closed it over one turgid peak.

Tina shook and shuddered, coming off the wall as he suckled her deep into his mouth. Pleasure forked down from the tips of her breasts to her pelvis in deep, sharp arrows. He pressed his tongue against the tip and began the torturous pleasure all over again. Just when she thought she couldn't bear it anymore, he started on the other breast.

The tremors coursing through her were constant now. Dampness coated her skin. His mouth still at her breast, he moved his hand down to her sex and penetrated her with a finger while his thumb pressed against her clit. Her head banged against the glass pane, Tina thrust her pelvis into his hand. Release was so close now, a shimmer of heat all over her skin, building and building.

"Open your eyes, *agapita*," Kairos whispered huskily. His words vibrated against her skin, pulling that knot in her belly tighter. "I know what brings you over the edge."

Tina looked down. His mouth was at her breast, his silver eyes darkened to a dark gray that happened only when he was aroused. His fingers didn't stop their rhythm but it was the heat in his gaze that pushed her. He rubbed his cheek against the wet, glistening nipple. His thumb and forefingers pinched her clit just as he commanded, "Come for me, Valentina."

Her orgasm broke over her, rolling and rippling through her in a flurry of waves that kept coming and coming. But he didn't stop. His fingers kept her at that high, riding that swollen, sensitive bundle.

The aftershocks shook her muscles until she flopped her forehead onto his shoulder and arrested his wrist. She felt boneless, as if she were nothing but a conduit for pleasure and sensations. "Stop, please, Kairos. No more."

His big hand remained between her thighs, soothing the tremors in her muscles. The other pushed back a damp tendril from her forehead. Tenderness. He'd always shown her tenderness in bed. For the span of a few minutes.

The last flutters of her release left her body, leaving an aching void behind. She'd challenged him so boldly that she would resist him. That she would never again fall into his arms. And here she was, her dress bunched up around her waist, against a glass wall while a crowd danced beneath them.

Still, there was a physical ache inside her where she wanted him. Needed him.

His mouth moved from her temple to her cheekbones to her jaw. His mouth was warm and hard, hungrier now. She thrust her tongue into his mouth, determined to pull him into the same sinking well of pleasure. He growled, his chest vibrating with it when she dug her teeth into his lower lip. Hard. And again.

He'd always controlled their sex life—when, where, how—all of it. Enslaved by the pleasure he gave, she'd allowed him to lead, blindly following. But no more.

Her hands automatically locked at his nape, pulling him closer.

His hard chest crushed her sensitive breasts.

His hands were filled with her buttocks. Lifting her against the glass, he brought her pelvis closer to his erection.

Moans erupted from their mouths as he rocked into her. Thick and long, his erection pressed against her sensitized clit, sending a quiet flutter of sensation through her again.

"Put your hands up."

A shiver went through her at the raw lust in the command. Denial whispered at her lips yet no words came out.

A rigid line to his mouth, he gripped her wrists and pulled her arms up. The arch of her spine pushed her breasts toward him. He didn't let go of her wrists. As if he didn't trust her. But his other hand, palm down, moved from her forehead to her nose, to her mouth.

When his fingers stilled at her lips, she instantly opened her mouth. She knew what he liked. He had trained her well enough. Though he had never let her take him in her mouth, even when she'd offered. But it wasn't just that he had taught her what pleased him.

She was addicted to his pleasure. Drunk on the power she felt for the few minutes when he needed her so desperately. When his control balanced on a serrated edge.

And she needed that tonight. She needed him to want her as desperately as she'd needed his touch.

His features hardened when she sucked his finger into her mouth. A shudder went through him at her caress. The raw pleasure etched on his hard, implacable features turned her on as if he had touched her again at her core.

She had lived for those moments. She took each callused finger into her mouth one after the other, knowing that it drove him crazy.

His silvery gaze devouring her, he undid the clasp of his belt buckle. The soft rip of the zipper punctured the sound of her harsh breaths. His trousers fell from his hips with a shy whisper.

She had no will left. Her gaze dipped down to his groin. Heat broke out over her skin again, instant, explosive, like lightning appearing over a dark sky in the blink of an eye. She stared, greedy for the sight of him.

Reaching out boldly, she pushed his shirt up until a patch of his ripped abdomen was visible. Dark skin stretched taut over defined musculature delineated with a line of hair. Even the V at the juncture of his groin was well defined.

His cock—she blushed at thinking the word he'd made her say in the second week of their marriage—thickened and lengthened under her hungry gaze, the soft head already glistening wet.

He hustled her back toward the glass again, his hands kneading her buttocks. His mouth buried in her neck again. Her nipples, hard once again, poked at his chest. His hands were everywhere. Even after he'd given her release, he wouldn't just take her. No, he built her body into a frenzy all over again.

If he had been a selfish lover, if he'd denied her pleasure even once, maybe she wouldn't have become such a slave to it. And to him. But no, he pushed her again and again to the edge. To release.

Rough hands pushed her dress all the way down. "I need to be inside you. Now. Valentina."

The question in his statement jerked her head up. He wouldn't assume, he wouldn't take.

"*No!*" The stillness that came over him had such restrained violence in it that she shivered.

In a fluid move, she sank to her knees.

His curse ripped the heavy silence when she wrapped her fingers around his hardness. Velvet-coated steel, he was so soft and yet so hard at the same time. His thigh muscles tensed like rocks when she braced her hands on them.

"Valentina, you don't—"

"Will you give up control for a few minutes? Will you let me in?"

She didn't wait for his answer. Bracing herself for the taste of him, she licked the soft head.

Salty and masculine. She looked up, her mouth open and ready. Tension etched onto every angle of his face. Such raw need and longing written on every hard plane of it that satisfaction pulsed through her.

Tilting her head down, she took him in her mouth this time. Another curse burst through the air. His hips jerked forward until he was filling her mouth.

Instantly, he pulled back. He was losing control. The thought spurred her on like a wild fire in the forest. *Bene,* she wanted him to lose control.

She repeated the movements of her mouth and hands. He said nothing, made no demands. When she glanced a look up at him, he growled an animalistic sound that sent shivers up and down her spine. But his body spoke for him. His hands had reached into her hair at some point. Every time she clasped him harder, he thrust a little into her mouth. Every time he hit the roof of her mouth, his thighs clenched a little more.

His body betrayed him, his need took over just as hers had done earlier. Using it, Tina sucked him harder, faster, intent on blowing his mind apart.

Her mouth felt hollow, her knees dug into the hard marble, her wrists were beginning to hurt from the repeated action but she didn't care.

Every discomfort was worth it for now her husband had no control left. His hands in her hair directed her mouth where and how he wanted it. Deeper and faster and harder.

And then suddenly, he pulled out of her mouth. Rough hands grasped her under her shoulders and pulled her up. She swayed, her knees shaky, and he held her fiercely close with one arm while he stroked himself.

His roar of pleasure vibrated around them as he came against her belly.

Tina looked up, a fever of arousal in her muscles at how completely undone he looked. Silence beat down around them, punctured only by his harsh breaths. His head bent against her shoulder, his breath hit her in warm strokes. His powerful body was still shuddering against hers.

She had no idea how long they stood like that. The scent of his release and hers cloyed the air, leaving her no escape from it. When he looked up at her, she closed her eyes. His thumb traced the line of her jaw softly, almost with reverence.

Her eyes flew open when she felt his fingers on her belly. He wiped her tummy with a napkin he produced from somewhere and then gently righted her dress. Heat swamped her cheeks.

His hands shook as he zipped up his trousers and buckled his belt. She tucked her hands to the side but the little tremors wouldn't subside.

She couldn't pretend that the whole experience hadn't shaken her. She truly was naive. Drawing satisfaction by seeing his control shatter, by bringing him to his knees like that, the raw intimacy of his actions…it had only seared him deeper into her psyche.

She looked away from him just as his gaze turned toward her. She walked over to the refrigerator on trembling legs and poured herself a glass of water. She drank the whole thing in one gulp, her mouth parched.

She felt him come to a stop right behind her. Hesitation, so uncharacteristic of him, charged the air. "Valentina—"

"Please, Kairos. Take me home."

He stared at her for what felt like an eternity before he nodded.

CHAPTER NINE

SHE HAD BARELY reached their room and changed out of the stupid dress, then come down for a cup of hot tea when he cornered her.

"I want to sleep. I'm… I can already feel the headache beginning."

He took hold of her wrist, tugging her into the study he had taken over from Theseus.

The smell of wood and cigars instantly reminded her of her grandfather Antonio. Another man who had thought she would amount to nothing.

While she stared into the empty fireplace, Kairos came back with steaming black coffee, cheese and perfectly cut apples.

"Eat."

Her stomach roiled so she took the plate from him and dutifully ate. He sat down on the step of the fireplace, his long legs bumping into hers until she shifted and the line of them grazed hers.

"Valentina, look at me."

Concern and something else glinted in his silver gaze. She forced a fake smile to her mouth. "My knees are a little the worse for wear, but, *si*, I'm perfectly fine."

He flinched then, whatever he saw in her eyes making him draw back. *As if she could hurt him!*

"I've never… I didn't ask you to do that for me."

"You did it for me." Just mentioning the day when he had put his mouth to the most intimate part of her sent shivers through her.

He scowled. "Why today?"

She looked at him and then away, afraid of what he would see in her eyes. "I was frustrated, feeling reckless." She looked down at her locked fingers. "The release you gave me took the edge off before I did something stupid. So I returned the favor."

A dangerous glint appeared in his eyes. One brow arched on his arrogant face. "Took the edge off? Was that what I did?"

His gaze dared her to shrug, to cheapen it.

He pinned her to the spot with his penetrating stare, as if he could see into her soul.

She swallowed and looked away. The endless silence, his painful indifference—it was all gone and there was a different man watching her. A man she'd always sensed beneath his ruthlessness but could never touch.

She struggled to make her voice casual. "Compared to my history of making a spectacle of myself every time I get upset, giving my almost separated husband a blow job is probably of minor consequence, *si*?"

"You do not fool me, Valentina. What happened at the nightclub couldn't have left you untouched—" he placed a broad palm over her chest "—in here."

Her heart pounded away under his touch. "Because only you can be casual about sex? Not I?"

"I've slept only with two women in my entire life. You and one other girlfriend. It was a convenient relationship I fell into and we went our separate ways when it wasn't more. I have never been casual about sex. I told you I don't fall into relationships easily. I had Theseus's support but when I left him, I had to start all over with little to my name. Careers like that don't leave room for relationships."

"You proposed to Sophia."

"Because I thought we would suit. Because we were friends and I admired her." He blew a breath, the light from the chandelier caressing his rugged features. "She was wiser than I was, which is why she said no. I realize now she had felt like a safe choice."

Every word out of his mouth mocked the wall she had erected.

She couldn't bear his tenderness, this concern. She couldn't fight her own need for him like this. Especially not today. "If I had known a blow job was all it would take to get you to open to me, I would have gone down on my knees long ago," she said flippantly.

When she would have shuffled away from him, he clasped her arms. "Stop being so glib! Stop acting as if that didn't mean anything."

"What did it mean then, Kairos?"

He looked as if she had slapped him, not asked a simple question. But when she thought he would shut down and walk away, he looked thoughtful. "It meant that you and I are not done with each other. And not just sexually. It meant that…this is not just about Helena and Theseus and our stupid deal or the divorce anymore. It is about us."

Her breath left her, her heart thudding against her ribcage. When he opened up like that, when he let her see what he was feeling, thinking, she… *No!* She couldn't.

Tina had never been so terrified by her own vulnerability, by her own stupid hope.

She wanted to break through the barriers he had erected between them, wanted to find the sweet man who had bought her a gift he knew she would love.

She wanted that Kairos in all the moments, not just every now and then. She would always want him. But would the way he saw her ever change? Could she give herself to him completely if he didn't respect her?

No. She couldn't.

She strolled onto the veranda, trying to get a grip on herself.

He settled down next to her on the small wicker sofa. Hesitation shimmered in his eyes. "I…shouldn't have kissed you today. I shouldn't have lost control. I want you every minute of every day. But only today I realized that what I… planned for you is wrong. What I thought about you is wrong."

"What did you plan for me?"

"I thought I would work you out of my system in these three months. I was angry… I felt betrayed when you left. My ego was definitely bruised."

Laughter burst out of her. "Oh, please…don't look so guilty. I meant to bring you to your knees by rubbing your nose in my fabulous self. I was going to make you regret ever leaving me."

Elbows on his knees, he bent forward. He sighed and studied his hands. One thick lock of hair fell forward onto his forehead, his shoulders bunched into a tight line. It was a rare glimpse into his true self that she couldn't help but drink in.

Her heart clenched when he looked up and smiled.

"I knew, even that night when I couldn't find you, that it wasn't just your fault our marriage had failed. I just…my pride wouldn't let me accept it, accept that while we both have flaws, what you gave me is priceless. You didn't throw it away on a whim or an impulse."

It felt as if they had reached a crossroads. "Look at us, all grown up, *si*?" she said trying to lighten the moment. "Being adult about a breakup. Maybe we can be friends like they show in American sitcoms?"

A blaze lit up in his eyes and she looked away.

Of course, it was a foolish suggestion. But the thought of having to walk away all over again, especially when she was finally getting to see beneath the rigid exterior…the very thought of it made her shiver.

"Will you please tell me what happened, Valentina?" He exhaled roughly. "I promise you I won't be cruel or mocking. I want to understand."

With one promise, he knocked all her barriers down. For Kairos never promised anything he didn't mean. "Chiara fired me. Only *I* could get fired from an unpaid internship, *si*?" The words fell over themselves to come out now.

"What? Today?"

"Right before you called me. I was…putting away my stuff. I feel like such a failure."

His arm came around her gently.

Tears pooled in her eyes and she inhaled noisily. "Don't be kind to me."

"What was the stupid thing you would have done today? Run away again?"

"Crawl back to my brothers. I miss them today." She swallowed the ache down. "I miss Leandro's tight hugs. Luca's corny jokes. I miss Alex's calm acceptance, Izzie's wet kisses. I miss Sophia's quiet support."

"They adore you, don't they?" he said softly.

"For years after Leandro brought me to live with them, every time something went wrong in my world, I would throw one hell of a tantrum." She laughed through the tears, realizing how insecure she'd been to doubt her brothers' love for her. "I'd push them to the edge as if to test them."

"To see how far you could push them before they rejected you? And if that was going to happen, you'd rather know sooner?"

The depth of his perception stunned her. "*Si*. If there's one thing I've learned through the debacle of our marriage, it's that I process everything that doesn't go my way by acting out. I think I did it at regular intervals—either when I thought Leandro was distant or when Luca disappeared for weeks. I would wreak hell and they would rush to reassure me that I was indeed loved and wanted. I was so…needy and vulnerable and they spoiled me to make up for losing my mother, for how terrified I had been when they found me after her death.

"There was nothing I wanted that couldn't be mine. Leandro even tried to protect me from the truth, *si*? And then I met you and you wouldn't dance to my tune…and all my insecurities came pouring out."

"Today, you wanted your brothers to tell you that it was okay to get fired at a job?"

"Yes. That I wasn't a useless waste of space. I wanted them to protect me from you."

He groaned and she laughed at the regret pinching his mouth. "I was such a—"

"Uptight, self-righteous ass?" she supplied. When he nodded and laughed, her heart slipped a little out of her reach. "Sophia's words."

"The last time I spoke to Chiara, she told me that your team all adore you. That you're taking them by storm."

She nodded. "I've been enjoying it. Chiara's not easy to work for but she's so talented. You were right, I was learning so much. We've been preparing for the fall collection. I've been liaising with designers and their assistants, and PR people to put a marketing campaign together. She let me put the outfits and accessories together. I even handpicked the models to showcase each different outfit. I talked to the photographers, the lighting assistants. A hundred different things have to come together perfectly for the collection to be showcased. I…honestly don't know how it happened. I double-checked and triple-checked everything. I spent most of the previous evenings calling every personal assistant and designer checking to make sure things would go smoothly. I…"

"What went wrong?"

"Honestly, I've no idea. I must have messed up something because we ended up with ten boxes of swimwear. Which is a *disaster* because it's October and the same order was shipped to about eleven different stores. Instead of Burberry coats, we have Bermuda shorts. Instead of designer pantsuits, we have sleeveless tops and shorts. Everything was wrong. The catalogs are not even ready. Chiara had a nightmare to fix on her hands and no inventory. Her phones kept going off. I tried to stem the panic from store managers waiting to figure out what to do. I… When I went into her office, one of the vice presidents was ripping into her. I told him it was my fault, not Chiara's. I… I quickly put together a letter of resignation and walked out."

"So she didn't really fire you then?"

He squeezed her fingers softly. "She was so buried that she didn't get a chance. We were alone for a moment in her office. She looked up and said she knew she shouldn't have taken me on. She knew I would only bring trouble."

"Valentina—"

"I… I had a simple job to do. And I messed it up." She rubbed the base of her palms around her eyes. "You were right. I should just accept that I'm not good for anything—"

Kairos tilted her chin up until she looked at him. "That's not true. I was a cruel bastard to say that." He'd always thought her weak-spined, a slave to suggestion, but only now could he see the strength that had always been there. "Valentina, listen to me. Making a mistake in a job is not the end of the world. What you do after is what matters. How many times you pick yourself up after you fall…that's what matters."

"Then I failed in that, too, *si*?" She laughed and the sound couldn't hide the frustration she felt. "Don't you see, Kairos? Letting you kiss me, touch me, letting myself get physically close to you…what I did today was not cheap, *no*. Was not meaningless. Seeing you undone—" her gaze landed on his mouth, his eyes, and he felt burned by the intensity of it "—it's a high I could chase again and again. But it is self-destructive behavior. It is harmful to me. *You are harmful to me.*

Every little bit of your past you give me, every small admission you make about what you feel for me…it comes at a high price. It comes with a fight, it feels like squeezing blood out of a stone. I think that's just how you're made. And if I've learned anything by watching my brothers and their wives, I know it shouldn't be this hard. You broke my heart last time and if I give you half a chance, you will do it again.

"So please…if you have ever cared for me, even a little bit, don't touch me. Don't kiss me." A ghost of a smile flitted over her face as her brown gaze moved over his. "Don't follow through on your nefarious plans."

"This…what happened between us tonight—" he moved his hand between them, a fine tension in his body "—is nothing shameful. This is not something that I would ever use against you."

"And yet this—my sexual desire for you—is what made you think I wouldn't hesitate before falling into another man's bed. That I would betray our vows."

He clasped her jaw, forcing her to look at him. "I was lashing out. I knew you wouldn't betray me. I just…on the best of days, you're like a hurricane. All I wanted was to contain you, contain the damage you did to—"

"Your reputation? Your business alliances?"

"Damn it, Valentina! *Damage to me!* To the way I wanted to live my life. I've never in my life cared about anyone. The only way I learned to survive was by being in control of myself. Even after I came to live with Theseus and Maria... I don't know how to let someone close. I don't know how to handle emotion and all that it entails. I can't bear the pain that comes from loving someone. I just...can't. And you...every day you made me insane. You mocked my rules, you teased my attention even when you weren't trying and when you got up to one of your spectacles, you threatened every ounce of my control."

"But you never lost it," she whispered, his confession searing through her.

Every time Kairos thought he had a grip on her, Valentina showed him a new side. Unraveled him anew. What they had done tonight at the nightclub had not just been physical release.

Christos, it only showed again how open she was. How much he could hurt her, if he wasn't careful.

And suddenly the idea of hurting Valentina was unconscionable.

"The more you pushed me for a reaction, I see now, the more I retreated. It became a matter of my will against yours. I couldn't…let you… have so much control over me. Being married to you—it was like asking a man who doesn't know how to walk to swim an ocean. You are right, though. It shouldn't be this hard. But I can't… I don't know if it will ever be different, either. I can't change what I am."

I won't love you.

Kairos knew she understood what he'd said because she paled and nodded. If there were tears in her eyes, she hid them by looking down at her clasped hands.

He should have felt an ease of the weight that had been cinching tight around his neck. Instead of relief that he had set the score right, that he had told her what the future could be, all he felt was an ache in his chest. An unnamed longing.

"The fault is not all yours, Kairos, I know that."

The vulnerability in her eyes, the lovely picture she made in the moonlight melted something near his heart. That she thought herself a failure because of his cruel words was unacceptable.

He knelt in front of her, took her hands in his, looked her in the eye. "I'm…sorry for making you feel like you're less than what you are. Even if Chiara fired you, you're not a failure. You're the most courageous woman I know. It took guts to walk away from your brothers, from me, from the lap of luxury. Guts to face all the people who mocked you, who treated you so horribly and to go to work at that place all these months. It took guts to try again and again to put together that blasted portfolio, guts to stand up to your black-mailing husband and make a deal of your own.

"You live your life with all your passion poured into it. You take risk after risk with yourself. And maybe there's no way forward for us, but *Christos,* I still want you. Desperately. Like I have never wanted anything else in life. But I won't touch you. Not unless your heart and mind both want me to."

Tina took a long, hot shower, took even longer to dress and finally walked back into the bedroom. She wasn't going to fall asleep anytime soon. She was too wired, too many thoughts whirling through her head. And she definitely didn't want to have the confrontation that was coming.

It was ironic since she'd always been the one that had pushed for it.

Since the nightclub a week ago, she'd been avoiding Kairos, faking sleep when he came to bed, running around the estate like the very devil was chasing her in the evening when he was home.

As always, he'd given it to her straight. Told her he would never change, never open himself up to her. Which should have sent her running for the hills.

Instead, his words seemed to have burrowed deep into her soul. She had seen the respect she'd wanted in his eyes. She'd seen the glitter of regret and pride when he had told her it had taken guts to stand up for herself.

That should have been enough. But all she wanted was more of him, more of the Kairos who saw the true her, the Kairos who kissed her as if he couldn't breathe, the Kairos who—

Dios, had she no self-preservation instinct?

"Couldn't hide any longer in the bathroom?"

Kairos's low voice halted her hand toweling her hair. She shrugged. Taking a deep breath, she finished brushing her hair, trying her hardest not to let her gaze settle on him in the mirror.

Turning to the dresser, she pulled out her running shorts, a T-shirt and a sports bra. She pulled her hair back into a high ponytail.

She barely took two steps before he was in front of her. Blocking her. Breath halted in her throat.

"Where are you going?"

She kept her gaze on his chest. The olive skin shadowed through his white dress shirt, which wasn't tucked quite neatly into his trousers. Every time she looked at him, she remembered him undone now. Heat swarmed her face again. *Dios*, what had she been thinking to be so…bold with him? That was a memory she wouldn't forget to her dying days. Nor did the image of him climaxing fail to arouse her. "I… I'm going for a run. I'm too restless to sleep."

"It's eleven thirty at night. And if you run anymore, you will disappear into thin air."

Before she could even blink, he took the clothes from her and threw them on the bed. A finger under her chin tilted her face up. "Is it working, Valentina?"

"What?"

"Avoiding me. Is it making the ache to be with me any less? Because if it is, you have to share the secret with me."

"I don't know... *No*. It is not helping. You're like that slice of chocolate cake that you can't resist even knowing that it will go to your hips and buttocks."

He laughed, lovely crease lines fanning out near his eyes. "I talked to Chiara today."

Hurt punched through her. "I can't go back to a job where not only am I not wanted, but can't even do anything properly, Kairos. How can I face my colleagues when they all see that I returned because of my powerful husband's recommendation? I will have no more value than a mannequin."

"Fine," he said, releasing her. Something like humor shone in his eyes. "Maybe I'm wrong in assuming you would want to hear what Chiara told me involved Helena."

Having dropped the bomb, the devilish man casually strolled to the balcony attached to the bedroom.

"What do you mean Helena was involved?"

"Sit down and maybe I will tell you."

She glared at him. And sat down.

He pulled her closer to him and she went unwillingly.

His thighs pressed against hers and instantly

that awareness slammed into her. But beneath that ever-present hum was something else, something new between them.

Tenderness. Rapport. The connection she had craved for so long with him. As if all the cacophony and noise in their relationship had been cleared away and they could see each other clearly for the first time.

And the more she saw of Kairos, the more Valentina liked him. Genuine like, not the I-want-to-rip-his-clothes-off kind. Although that was there, too.

"I have been thinking on what you said to me."

Instantly, he tensed. "Which part?"

Tina could literally feel his stillness. The way it contained his rumbling emotions. He thought she had made a decision about them, their future. And he was hanging on an edge just as she was any time she thought about it. "About picking myself up, planning my next move. I will find another way to achieve my goals. Working with Chiara gave me the confidence that I'm in the right field, that I can work as hard as it takes. That I have a natural talent for fashion. It's just a matter of finding the right outlet, the right opportunity."

The smile he shot her was full of joy and admiration. "I'm glad to hear that."

"So…anyway, *efharisto*, Kairos."

"You needn't thank me, I did nothing."

"Thank you for seeing me through that first hurdle. For…just being there." And since she had to fight the glittering desire she saw in his eyes, she quipped, "For showing me that when I hit the next hurdle, all I have to do is get drunk, go to a nightclub and maybe find a guy to—"

"You finish that sentence at serious threat of harm to yourself, Valentina."

His growl made laughter explode from her mouth. She leaned back into her seat, and took a deep breath of the scented air.

When Kairos had handed her a glass of red wine, she took a sip and sighed.

"No more than one glass," she added.

He smiled, slanted a teasing, hot glance her way. "I was hoping you wouldn't count. I was hoping to get you drunk and have my wicked way with you. I like you drunk."

"Ha ha…not funny. You like what I do when I'm drunk." *Dios mio*, he was even more irresistible when he teased her like that.

"Too horny for it to be a joke?" There was a

flash of his white teeth and that rakish smile. Tina wondered if her panties could melt by how hot and wet she was.

"Something like that, *si*," she replied haughtily and had the pleasure of being enveloped by his deep laughter again.

"I have always loved your honesty, *agapita*." Her heart thudded against her ribcage. "Fine, no more than one glass."

As far as the eye could see, darkness blanketed the grounds. Crickets chirped. The scents of pine and ocean created a pungent yet pleasant perfume on the air. For a long while, neither of them spoke.

His arm came around her shoulders, his fingers drawing lazy circles on her bare skin. There was nothing sexual about his touch and still her breath hung on a serrated edge. The intimacy of the moment was even more raw than what they had shared at the nightclub.

"Do you realize we've never once…spent time like this? Without fighting, without ripping each other's clothes off?" The words escaped her—wistful, poignant—before she could lock them away.

Moonlight threw shadows on her hand clasped

in his. His thumb passed back and forth over the veins on the back of her hand. She sensed he was as loath to disturb the moment as she was. "Hmmm. Although I always liked the ripping-clothes-off part, too."

She snorted and he snorted back.

"Today is my mother's birthday," he said suddenly into the silence.

"I…do you miss her?"

"Yes. She would have liked you. She was like you—fierce, bold."

She laced her fingers through his and brought his hand to her mouth, pressing a soft kiss to the veins on the back of his hand. Strength and willpower and vulnerability—she was only beginning to realize what a complex man he was.

"I would like to know more about her, please."

He remained quiet for so long that Tina sighed. She couldn't force him to share pieces of himself with her. She couldn't forever be the one who took that first step. Not because of pride but because she couldn't bear the hurt of it when he left her standing again.

Until he started speaking. "She was a prostitute. I know how they're forced into those choices firsthand, the wretchedness of that life. She fed me from the money she made through her…job. Until she fell sick and drifted into nothing."

Even in the slivers of moonlight, Kairos saw how pale Valentina became. She blinked until the sheen of tears dimmed. Only then did he realize he'd revealed something he'd told only one other person. Theseus.

"I'm sorry that you…"

"That I came from such a dirty past?"

"That you lost a mother you loved." Pure steel filled her voice, daring him to mock her sympathy. "No matter her choices. I know what it feels like to lose a loved one."

Why did he forget that beneath the sophistication and good humor, Valentina's childhood hadn't been smooth, either? That she, more than anyone, understood the ache that came with loving someone?

It was as if he still, willingly, refused to look beneath the impulsive, reckless woman he had initially assumed she was.

"Are you ashamed of who she was?" The question was soft, tentative.

He scowled. "No. Never. Why the hell would you think that?"

"Because," she said with a sigh, "you play your

cards pretty close to your chest, Kairos. Even when they did that exposé on you for that business magazine, there was nothing about your background. Top businessman under thirty and it was as if you had sprouted from nowhere as a full-grown businessman at the age of twenty-three."

He grimaced, recognizing the truth in Valentina's summation.

The journalist who'd done that interview had been so frustrated. More than once, she'd tried to steer the conversation to his childhood and he'd bluntly steered her away, keeping his answers to his successes and the companies he had fixed.

He wasn't ashamed, but for years, he *had* hidden his roots. He'd pushed away men who could have been friends because he'd felt separate, isolated. Felt as if he hadn't belonged because of where he had come from.

His mind whirled as thoughts poured through him.

"How did you come to live with Theseus and Maria?"

He braced himself, knowing what it was building to. Knowing that Valentina wouldn't stop until all of him was stripped before her. His illusions and his control. "He and Maria came to one of the most impoverished areas of Athens and he caught me as I cut the strings to Maria's purse and started running."

He heard her soft gasp and clenched his heart—or what remained of it—against the pity. Memories came at him like swarming bees. The poverty. The filth. The fight to survive another day. As if she was losing him to the past, Valentina tightened her fingers around his, brushed a soft kiss against the underside of his jaw.

"Do not pity me, Valentina. This is why I wouldn't reveal my background before. Because it skews people's perception of me. Instead of a powerful businessman, they see a man who's crippled by his roots."

She snuggled into him as if he hadn't just snarled at her. "Or they see a man who made something of himself even when the odds were stacked against him. You keep treating me as if I'm unfamiliar with anything in life but designer couture and privilege, Kairos. If Leandro hadn't persuaded Antonio that I belonged with them, if he hadn't found me and brought me to live with him and Luca, where do you think I would be today? You think I've forgotten the fear that no one will care about me. Just because I pretend as if that doesn't matter it doesn't mean it's not there every day within me."

He looked at her and this time only saw understanding. Again, the realization, that this understanding had always been there for him to reach for, filled him.

The realization that Valentina was more than he'd ever wanted in a wife. It was as if his subconscious had been aware of it all along.

Was that why he'd always kept her at a distance? Why he'd retreated in the face of her passionate declarations, treated her with cold indifference?

She cupped his palm tenderly, her thumb tracing his jawline back and forth. It was comfort, it was affection. And still the jolt of that contact rang through him. Neither was he unaware of the different kind of intimacy the night and their discussion had wrought on them.

She was stealing away pieces of him. He tried to fight it, a sense of dread blanketing him, but her tender touch anchored him to the here, to the now. To her.

"How old were you?"

"Eleven? Twelve?" He rubbed his free hand

over his face. "I was this…feral animal that would have done anything to survive another day. I was terrified he'd turn me in to the police. Theseus was really built in those days. He restrained me for fifteen minutes while I tried to break his hold and run. I stopped fighting when he said he would not turn me in. I was shocked when he brought me to his home. That first year I was terrified he would change his mind and throw me out. By the time, I was thirteen, Theseus and Maria adopted me officially."

"Then why did you leave them?"

The question came at Kairos like a fist, smashing through the walls he hadn't even known he'd need against her. "You know the answer to that."

"*No*, I don't." Something almost akin to desperation rang in her voice. "All I have is conjecture based on the little tidbits Helena hints at. Based on what you show me and the world at large."

Jaw tight, he stared at Valentina. Felt a visceral tug at the genuine concern in her eyes. Not pity. Not disgust. But a real emotion that had always been there. That he chose not to embrace, not to want.

He still couldn't make himself want it. If he

went that last step... "It was time to see the world, time to stretch my wings. To reach for bigger and greater things."

"You mean find a richer and maybe slightly less crazy heiress compared to Helena?"

He laughed. And she laughed. But they both knew he was skating over the issue. A part of him wanted her to push, like she did, relentlessly. One part of him wanted never to see her again.

It was the same torment he faced night after night.

Every cell in him wanted to tie Valentina to his side. To seduce her, to chain her to him with his touch, to promise her whatever she wanted. To build a family with her, to fill his life with laughter and drama and everything she brought into it. He wanted to be selfish and take what he wanted, despite the aching vulnerability in her eyes.

Another part of him cringed at the very idea, his self-preservation instinct coming to the fore. His subconscious had known even back then.

Valentina was dangerous to him. She would send him down a path where only pain waited.

And soon he was going to have to make a decision. For he had no doubt that she would leave him when their deal was up if he didn't reach for her.

The idea of Valentina forever walking out on him this time…he couldn't bear it.

CHAPTER TEN

TINA HAD PLANNED on escaping the party Kairos and Helena had arranged to celebrate Theseus and Maria's fiftieth wedding anniversary by hiding behind her workaholic boss.

The truth was that she was afraid to face what was happening between her and Kairos. To face what was happening to her.

After he had told her how Helena was the one who had messed up the purchase orders—something Chiara had realized from the beginning—she had returned to work. Despite Kairos's worry that Helena's antics were escalating and against his wishes.

Of course, he hadn't let her confront Helena.

Loath to disturb the truce they seemed to have achieved, she had quietly gone back to work.

Seeing him night after night stretched her nerves to the end. They couldn't look at each other without plunging into sexual tension. It was like waiting for a rumbling volcano to erupt. She sensed his hesitation, too, the way he studied her as if he wanted to devour her, the way he barely even touched her, as if his control were hanging by a thread.

The way he talked about everything but the future.

There was a friendship of sorts between them, however much he didn't like the label. They talked about her job, his work, about mutual friends. About their livelihoods.

She wanted to hide tonight. From him, from Theseus and Maria and Helena and from every board member that wanted to meet Valentina Constantinou.

She wanted the world to disappear and leave her alone with Kairos so that she could...

She could what? Figure out where it was that they were heading? Figure out if she wanted to take a step toward him again?

Was she willing to put herself through all that heartache again? Was she prepared to wait forever if she wanted him to take that step toward her?

Kairos had, of course, in his usual commanding tone ordered Tina's presence at the party. She was, he'd decreed this morning over breakfast, required as his wife.

Keep up your side of the bargain, Valentina, were his parting words without so much as a look in her direction. He hadn't even taken her calls the rest of the day so she couldn't offer him excuses.

In the end, she'd decided she didn't want another argument with him. She didn't want to push him for she had a feeling they were both treading a fine line.

She arrived at Markos Villa with the dress and shoes she'd purchased with his credit card on her lunch break, to find a mass of activity in the huge acreage behind the villa.

Sunset was still a couple of hours away but the orange light lent a golden glow to the white silk marquees being put up. Tables were being dressed with lanterns and orchids in little glass jars. An extensive wine bar was set up on one end while a small wooden dance floor had been erected in the middle of all the small tents.

Fifty years! Theseus and Maria were celebrating fifty years of marriage. Of being together, of knowing one another inside out. Of belonging to one another.

Something she still wanted with the Kairos she was slowly discovering.

With a sigh, she made her way up the stairs outside the villa.

An eerie calm dwelled inside the high-ceilinged walls, in contrast to the hubbub of activity outside. A line of sweat poured down between her shoulder blades. Something felt wrong. As she walked through the airy villa, poured herself a glass of water in the kitchen, the sense of unease only got stronger.

Where were Theseus and Maria and Helena?

Apprehension sitting like lead in her gut, Tina took the stairs up. Suddenly, all she wanted was to see Kairos. To reassure herself that he was okay. On the first-floor landing, she was walking past the main master suite—Theseus and Maria's rooms—when she heard the argument.

She hadn't meant to pause and overhear, but over the last month, she had only become more and more attached to the older couple. Whatever the tension between their daughter, Kairos and them, there was a bond of steel between the husband and wife. An unshakeable love that Tina wanted in her own life. A bond made of respect, humor and utter affection. She'd even wondered how such a lovely couple could have given birth to such a brittle woman like Helena. She wouldn't have dreamed of eavesdropping but it was Maria's voice raised, close to breaking, and uttering Kairos's name that halted her steps.

She had a good grasp of Greek now and yet Maria's impassioned argument was hard to follow. She was imploring Theseus not to cut their own daughter out. To give Helena one more chance to prove the truth? To come to see the proof of it with his own eyes.

Kairos's true nature? Proof?

Wait, Theseus was going to cut Helena out of the company? How could he do that to his own daughter? Had Kairos persuaded him to it finally?

Tina's thoughts whirled and collided, a cold chill sweeping over her skin. What kind of proof was Maria talking about? What did Helena mean to prove to her parents?

She had tried to fill Valentina's mind with the supposed love between Kairos and her. It hadn't worked. She had tried to get her to leave by ruining her work. It hadn't worked.

What new scheme was she cooking now?

Heart racing a thousand miles a minute, Tina reached the vast bedroom she'd been sharing with Kairos. She dropped the bags on the floor, her gaze sweeping over the furniture and contents.

Kairos's huge desk was littered with papers, as was customary, but nothing seemed out of place. She could hear the shower running. And then she saw it—a flash of blue silk from the connecting door that led to the shared veranda. The other door from the veranda, she'd discovered the first evening, led to Helena's bedroom.

When she'd laughingly inquired of Theseus, he had told her that the house had been originally designed for a husband and a wife to share different bedrooms. With a wink at Kairos, the older man had gruffly announced he'd never want Maria to sleep in a separate bedroom. Maria had charmingly blushed.

Tina knew who would walk in to their bedroom in a few seconds. She could already hear the gruff baritone of Theseus's voice and Maria's pleading one—still close to tears. She didn't wait to see who would emerge from the veranda.

Unbuttoning her dress shirt, she pushed it off her shoulders. Next her trousers. By the time she reached the huge, rectangular glass-enclosed shower, she was in matching black bra and lace panties. The shape of a muscular flank made her hesitate.

With a deep breath, she pulled off her bra, then pushed down her panties and entered the shower.

To say her husband was stunned would have been the understatement of the year. To say she had forgotten how the sight of his naked body made her feel would be the understatement of the century.

All she could do was stare at him.

Water poured down Kairos's muscular body in rivulets. His dark hair pasted to his scalp made his rugged features harsher. His nose was broken and bent. His mouth a wide, cruel line. His neck was corded and muscled. Every inch of him was a feast to her starving senses.

Sparse hair covered a broad chest. His skin was like rough velvet—a sharp contrast to her own soft skin.

A line of hair arrowed down over his ridged abdomen, becoming thicker near his hips and then his pelvis. Legs built like a gladiator's clenched at her leisurely perusal.

Then, and only then, did she let her gaze drift

to his arousal. He lengthened and hardened until it was curved up toward his belly.

A soft moan flitted from her mouth as she remembered the sensation of him moving inside her. For a man who didn't dance, he made love with a sensuality that made her eyes roll.

"If you don't stop looking at me like that, I will be inside you in two seconds. I will not give a damn if it is harmful or a weakness or what promises you drew from me." He sounded ragged, at the end of his rope. "I'm but a man, Valentina."

Her skin prickling, she pulled her gaze to his. The heat she saw there blasted through her meager defenses. Her nipples tightened into painful points, her breasts ached to be cupped.

Her breath came in serrated puffs as his gaze took in the plump points of her nipples, down her midriff to the junction of her thighs where wetness suddenly rushed, the scent coating the moisture-laden air around them.

Legs trembling, Tina turned away.

One more second of his gaze traveling down her length and she would have begged him to take her.

From the moment he'd slowly peeled off her

wedding dress on that night, she'd realized she loved sex. That she had an appetite to match his own voracious one. And yet today, enclosed in the glass cubicle with his hard body mere fingertips away, all she felt was a longing. To belong to him. To possess him in equal measure—mind, body and soul.

To love him for the rest of their lives.

She touched her forehead to the glass wall, hoping to cool off. Willing her body to find a thread of reason as to why this wasn't a good idea.

She felt him move in the small space. He didn't touch her yet the heat radiating from his body was like a blanket over her skin.

"Valentina?" In his husky voice, her name was both an order and a request. He touched her then, his palm around her neck, while his other hand traveled down her bare back to her spine. To her hips.

With a deep groan, he pulled her closer, until his erection settled against her buttocks. Their guttural gasps rent the air.

"Wait," she managed, the scrape of his chest against her tightening her hunger.

"Now who's punishing whom, *pethi mou*?"

"I would never tease you like that," she whispered hurriedly. "She…planned something, Kairos. I don't know what. I just couldn't… I couldn't let them think that of you."

Instantly, she felt the change in the air. He was still warm and hard but it was as if he had turned off a switch. "Who planned what?"

She didn't have to answer the question. They could hear voices just outside the bathroom—Maria urging Theseus.

The silence raging behind her had such a dangerous quality to it that she turned.

Rage filled Kairos's face, making it so harsh that Valentina instantly clasped his cheeks. What could she say? What platitude could she offer when she had willfully believed the worst of him? Wouldn't she have believed her own eyes, too, if she'd been but a few minutes late?

He pushed her palms away as if they burned him. Cold dawned into his silver eyes, making them into a winter wasteland. "Did you see her?"

Valentina shook her head. "Only a flash of her dress. That turquoise blue silk she'd chosen for tonight."

He said nothing in reply.

Valentina shut the shower off and grabbed the

towel from behind her. "I will go out first," she said softly, afraid of touching him.

He wouldn't harm Helena however angry he got, but she was also aware of his struggle to control his temper. She'd never seen him like this, so ragged at the edges.

What Helena had attempted to do, what Theseus and Maria would have seen if Valentina hadn't acted quickly...it was dirty, disgusting. And it had shaken him to the core.

She could see his frustration, his anger, but also for the first time since she'd met him, the depth of his affection for Theseus. He loved that old man and his wife. It was written in the torment on his face.

Becoming the company's CEO meant nothing to him. Only Theseus's love, his good opinion of him mattered.

It would have hurt him immeasurably if Theseus and Maria had found him in the shower with Helena. Finally—a true glimpse of the man she had married. A deeply caring man beneath the hard shell, the ruthless ambition.

All she felt were his emotions—raw and bleeding in that moment. And her own answering ones—desperate and potent. Everything to do with him and not her.

It was the first time in her life Tina felt someone else's pain. The first time she felt this overwhelming urge to reach out. To do anything she could to take that pain from him.

She wanted to hold him and never let go. But she understood him now. He would reject any comfort she offered. "Don't…do not embarrass them," he said between gritted teeth.

Confused for a few seconds, she stared at him. Then nodded, another realization hurtling through her.

He would do anything to protect them from embarrassment, from hurt. Even if it was heaped upon them by their own daughter. He would go to any lengths to hide Helena's reality from Theseus, to protect Theseus.

Even pretending to love the impulsive, juvenile wife that had walked out on him without doing the courtesy of telling him face to face.

She wrapped the towel around herself, pasted a smile to her face and stepped out. The pristine marble tiles were cold beneath her feet, jerking her into this moment.

Grabbing a smaller towel, she wiped the water

dripping from her hair. Took a few deep breaths to clear the lump from her throat. Forced a cheery tone into her voice and said loudly, "Wait until you see my dress, Kairos. You're not going to want to leave the bedroom."

CHAPTER ELEVEN

ALL THROUGH THE party Tina waited for the explosion of Kairos's temper to come.

Maybe not in front of Theseus and Maria. It was after all their wedding anniversary celebration.

Maybe not in front of the guests who were extended family and board members from the Markos company and even employees and their families.

But in private maybe. Just between them? Would he confront Helena at least to see if what they'd assumed was right?

No!

Her husband acted as if nothing untoward had happened.

Helena appeared a few minutes after her parents and Kairos and Valentina had started welcoming the guests together.

Like a queen finally drifting down to meet her

citizens. Like she hadn't tried to spread poison among people who cared about her.

Kairos's fingers clamped tight around her bare arm. "Stay out of this, Valentina."

Her hackles rose at his whispered warning. "But she—"

His fingers drifted to her hips, his grip so tight as he turned her that she had to smother a pained gasp. Instantly, he released her, a flash of something in the silvery gaze. "It doesn't concern you."

"How can you say that? If I hadn't—"

"You played the role I brought you here for, *ne*? You went out of your way to keep up your side of the bargain. For that I thank you. But Helena is my business and mine alone."

Hurt festered like an unhealed wound but for once in her life, Tina tried to put her own hurt aside for a moment and think of him.

He was in pain and he was lashing out at her. But she wouldn't let him. She wouldn't let him shut her out again. With all the guests' gazes on them, she clasped his jaw and pulled him until his mouth was a bare inch from her. Until he was all she saw, all she felt. Until everything she felt was mirrored in her gaze.

Until there was no escape from the truth in her eyes. "I did it because I care about you, because I couldn't bear to see you hurt. Don't shut me out tonight, not after everything we have shared the last couple of months. Please, Kairos. Don't turn away from me. From us."

She didn't wait for his reply. She had said what she meant to say, what she meant to do.

Helena was dressed in an exquisite blue, knee-length cocktail dress that made her look like a voluptuous baby doll. A diamond choker glittered at her throat. She looked innocent, beautiful—a façade.

Tina smoothed a hand down her own emerald green dress that left her shoulders bare and fell to her ankles, with a slit on one side. Her hair—since she hadn't even washed it properly in that shower—was neatly tied into a French braid.

Much as she tried to separate herself from the occasion and the people, Tina was drawn into the warmth of the celebration. She danced with Theseus, another older man with a bulbous face and kind eyes, a younger man who told her in Greek she was beautiful and that Kairos didn't deserve two beautiful women drifting about him.

Kairos had danced with Maria first, and then

he'd twirled Helena around the dance floor. Which had lasted four minutes and fifty-two seconds, too.

But he hadn't asked her. He'd watched her all evening with that consuming gaze—until Tina had felt as if she were standing naked in front of him again. As if he was testing her words, as if he didn't trust them. As if he loathed believing her.

Defiant and resolved, she met his gaze every time he looked at her. Let him see that this time she wasn't backing out, let him see the decision she had already made. The awareness between them was underscored by something heavier, darker.

Soon, she was surrounded by both men and women as she regaled them with the stories of growing up around her powerful brothers.

Unlike Conti Luxury Goods, however—which was a much more powerful and bigger conglomerate than the Markos Group, thanks to Leandro—Theseus's company was smaller and possessed a close-knit community feeling. Most of the board members and employees had been with the company for over twenty or even thirty years. And intensely loyal to Theseus, which made the attempted hostile takeover that much worse.

Even after a gap of seven years—Kairos had left when he'd been twenty-one—their trust and confidence in him was absolute. That he would naturally succeed Theseus as the CEO a foregone conclusion. She heard tales of Kairos's kindness, his leadership, his work ethic as he'd learned the ropes of the business under Theseus's guidance. Something she had learned herself in the last few weeks.

As night drove away the remnants of the lovely day, small lanterns lit on the tables threw faces into shadows. Strings of lights illuminated the grounds, marking paths.

Dinner was a lavish affair, with guests calling out for speeches. Theseus made one about Maria while she looked up at him adoringly and smiled. Helena made one, though it was mostly about the legacy Theseus would leave, as if he were already gone.

When Kairos raised his glass, a palpable hush fell over the crowd. "To Theseus and Maria…you are…" His Adam's apple bobbed up and down. Clearly, he was battling with his own emotions. "To another fifty years," he finished simply.

Maria burst into tears, her arms loosely wrapped around Kairos's waist from the side. The entire party came to a silence as if the moment were frozen in time. Helena frowned. Theseus kept his hand on his wife's back, concern lighting his eyes.

But it was Kairos's reaction that made Tina's chest so tight that she could barely breathe.

He had become utterly still the moment Maria had wrapped her arms around him. His shoulders painfully rigid, his jaw so tight that he might have been cast from marble. Only his eyes glittered with such raw emotion, such depth of pain that Tina had to look away. Seconds piled on into minutes as Maria silently sobbed, her face buried in Kairos's chest.

Tina took his free hand in hers and shook him slightly. "Kairos?"

Awakening from whatever held him in its ragged grip, Kairos awkwardly patted Maria's back while Theseus pulled her to him.

Theseus stood up again, raised his wineglass and announced his retirement. A pin dropped could have sounded like thunder in the thick silence.

"It is something I should've done years ago,"

he said, holding Kairos's gaze, an apology and something else in his tone. "I announce Kairos Constantinou as the new CEO of the Markos group of companies."

Applause thundered around them and yet as she saw Helena's face, dread curled around Tina's spine.

Helena hated Kairos and the depth of it terrified Tina. But even beneath that fear throbbed the sinking realization that he had what he wanted.

He was the CEO.

Which meant he had no need of Tina anymore.

While she…she had only just realized how desperately she was in love with him.

Midnight had come and gone by the time Tina went upstairs. Theseus had tired soon and Tina had convinced him and Maria to retire. Since Helena had been missing in action for several hours, she had taken over as the hostess. And stayed with a smile on her face until the last guest had departed.

But now as she dragged herself up the stairs, her feet hurt and a headache was beginning to throb at her temples. The staff had already cleaned up most of the debris from the party. Utter silence reigned over the villa.

Kairos was nowhere to be seen.

She took a quick shower and dressed in pajamas. Urgency and anxiety together made a nasty cocktail in her head. But she held onto the belief that he would come to her. He had to. He felt something for her and she would make that enough. She would make it work. They belonged together.

She drifted into sleep, the same thought running circles around her head.

Tina awoke suddenly, consumed with a feverish sense of urgency.

Pure darkness blanketed the room. The curtains that would have let in the moonlight were closed. Her skin prickled with awareness. She scooted up in the bed and turned on the lamp on the night stand.

Kairos was seated in the armchair in the corner. A bottle of whiskey lay unstoppered next to him. Half empty. And no glass. Tall legs stretched in front of him drew her gaze to his muscular thighs. His tie was gone. Jacket discarded.

The white shirt was unbuttoned all the way

to his abdomen. Golden olive skin dotted with sparse dark hair beckoned her touch.

And yet it was his face, wreathed in shadows, that drew her breath in serrated puffs. Dark brows winged over deep-set silver eyes perfectly framing his face. The thin, cruel slash that was his mouth. The strong column of his throat. His nostrils flared as he seemed to wait for her to acknowledge him.

"Kairos?"

"Your negligee is loose."

"What?" It took her a few seconds to comprehend his words. Heat swarming her cheeks, she tugged the strap that had fallen off her shoulder, baring most of her breast. "What are you doing here?"

"I'm not allowed in our bedroom?"

"Of course you are," she said, swallowing down the panic rising through her. Something was wrong. The way he stared at her, the stillness… He hadn't looked like that even when she'd told him what Helena had planned. Now…whatever had happened in the evening since, he looked unraveled. Completely undone.

And yet he had sought her out. He had been

waiting for her in the dark, pain etched on every feature.

"I meant, why are you sitting there? In the darkness. Alone."

His tongue flicked over his lower lip. Her pulse raced. He stared at her for a long time before he responded. "I was wondering if I should wake you or not."

"Wake me?" she repeated, still grappling with the dangerous quality surrounding him. It seemed as if her mind couldn't concentrate on his words. Only on the vibe that radiated from him. "Is something wrong with Theseus or Maria? She did seem off all evening, I wondered if she was ill or if…"

Her words fell away as she reached him. Something about his stillness discouraged touch. Her hands hung loosely at her sides.

Silvery eyes raked down the length of her with a thoroughly possessive intent. She hadn't brushed out her hair before falling into bed. Now her braid was half undone, thick strands falling over her shoulders.

The negligee she'd picked was one she had bought after their wedding, a soft pink silk that hung loose around her chest now. Falling several inches above her knees, however, it bared most of her thighs and legs.

A sharp laugh from him startled her and she instinctively jumped back.

Her hand shot to her chest, rising and falling heavily. "What is funny?"

"Your legs."

"My legs are funny?"

"Did you pick that negligee on purpose?"

Her cheeks heated as the memory of all the provocative nightwear she'd worn to entice him. "I…was too exhausted and honestly I didn't think you'd be coming to bed anytime soon."

"You make it hard, Tina. You always make it so damn hard," he whispered, almost to himself.

She could no more stop her gaze from moving to his crotch than she could stop breathing. The shape of his arousal spiked her heartbeat.

He laughed, again, and she hurriedly pulled up her gaze to his. "That, too, *glykia mou.*" Wicked lights danced in his eyes. "I always rise to the occasion, *ne*?"

"*Si*, always."

It was impossible not to laugh, even in the fraught moment. He looked young and charming and careless then, as if the tight grip he held over himself had snapped finally. It was a stark contest to the focused, always strategizing man she'd come to know.

What had snapped it?

"Kairos, how much have you drunk?"

Without answering her, he took the heavy bottle and took a huge gulp again. "You don't drink," she said softly.

"Usually, I don't. My mother…" His words didn't quite slur, though he seemed to lose focus. "I told you about her, *ne*?"

Her throat burned at the affection in his voice. "*Si*, you did."

"She hated what she was forced to do to…feed me. So every evening, as she got ready for work, she would drink. She would drink after she came back. For years, she drank to drown out her reality. In the end, her liver was so damaged that she drifted away into nothing. I hate alcohol. How it promises to dull things down and yet it doesn't."

He stared at the bottle in his hand, and plunked it down with such force on the side table that the thick glass instantly shattered, and his hand plunged into the broken shards with the force of it.

Valentina gasped and reached for him.

"*Oxhi, Valentina*!" His hands held her hips in a bruising grip. "There are shards everywhere. Your feet are bare."

Blood from the cut on his hand painted his shirt. "Kairos?"

"Yes, *agapita*?"

"Your hand...will you please let me dress it?"

He nodded and released her.

Tina darted into the bathroom, and came back with the first-aid kit. In silence that pulled her nerves, she finished dressing the deep cut, and wound it with gauze. She put the kit away, and pushed the broken fragments under the table and stared down at him.

He was staring at her as if he meant to devour her. And didn't know where to begin.

She was arrested between his wide legs, his face scant inches from her belly. Heat from his body hit her in powerful waves, the thin silk of her negligee no barrier.

"*Christos*, you smell like heaven," he said, pulling her closer. "Like you're the only place I can land, Valentina. But that is a mirage, too, *ne*? You're dangerous, *glykia mou*. Always a threat to my sanity."

Tina sank her hands into his hair to steady herself while he buried his face in her belly. He nuzzled her, as if he meant to burrow into her, setting every nerve ending on fire.

"Kairos?"

"I need you, *agapita*. So badly… I need you tonight." There was a ragged question underneath the demand that twisted her heart. He was not sure of her and she had only herself to blame for it.

"I'm here, Kairos. I've always been here, for you."

But there was no tenderness left in the moment. No humor. Only his need. Only the pain in his eyes and the frantic urgency she felt in his breath, in his movements to escape it.

His hands circled her waist restlessly, settling on her buttocks, and pressed her harder into his face. Molten heat spread from his mouth. The wet patch stuck to her skin. A heaviness filled her breasts, pooling into damp warmth at the juncture of her legs. The tension in his frame multiplied as he held her like that.

Then his hands were teasing the backs of her legs and thighs. Sneaking under the silky hem, cupping her buttocks, dragging her higher up against him. Higher, higher, lifting her with those sinewy arms. Until she was half standing, half draped over his shoulders.

Until his face was flush with her mound.

Tina swallowed the sound that rose to her lips, her trust absolute. Willing him to take whatever he needed.

His hot breath fell in puffs against her.

She jerked at the sudden surge of sensation so sharp that she almost fell backwards. But he didn't release her. He held her as if he would never let go.

As if she were his salvation.

Her fingers crawled from his hair to his neck. When he pressed a warm, wicked kiss against the silk pooling at her sex, she dug her nails into his neck.

He growled and burrowed his mouth into her folds. Her spine arched, the knot in her lower belly so tightly wound. Her breath became fire. His fingers bit into her hips, the pain coating the pleasure with a sharp contrast that made it unbearable.

A thousand little tremors exploded when he opened his mouth, when his teeth dug into the lips of her sex. Violent shivers that she couldn't contain. Moans and whimpers that she couldn't swallow. Up, up, up went the silk. Until she was bared to him utterly and there was not even a flimsy barrier between his wicked mouth and her willing flesh.

Rough fingers dragged over her hips, her buttocks, stroking, kneading, clutching. No thoughts marred the pure lights of sensation darting up and down her body.

And then his tongue was there at the place where she ached for him. Always. Stroking, licking, laving. Pushing her higher, higher, higher onto the cliff. Driving away everything else from her body except him, and what his mouth, and his wicked tongue did to her.

Insistent. Raw. Relentless. She moaned and rocked into his mouth, clutching onto him as if he were her everything.

She was transported to that wanton place only Kairos could take her. And then the knot in her belly broke apart, her muscles clenched long and deep, pleasure splintering through her. Her thighs shook from the pressure, every inch of her trembling.

Arching into the warmth of his body, she pulled the negligee off and threw it away. His cheeks were flushed with stripes of color. Fingers trembling, she somehow undid the clasp of his belt. Unzipped his trousers. And then he was in her palm. Hard and hot. Thick. Lengthening.

"Inside you, Valentina, now." The open need in his words was a balm to her soul.

Straddling his thighs that spread her indecently wide, she pushed down. His hips jerked up, and he thrust into her with one smooth stroke, fingers holding her hips grounded against him.

A long curse ripped out from his sinful mouth.

Tina gasped. Her body felt invaded even after the release he had given her, shivers of a different kind building over her skin. He was so deep. So hard inside her. Entrenched inside her body just as he always was in her heart.

A slow panic began to build inside her. She would never be free of him now. Never come out of this intact if he pushed her away.

"Shh...*agapi mou*..." he whispered against her temple. Long fingers stroked her damp skin softly. Soothingly. Until the tremors quieted.

A soft kiss against her damp lips. A featherlight stroke against her cheek. He nuzzled his stubble into her neck as if he had all the time in the world. As if just being inside her was enough.

"I didn't forget for one second how tight you

feel around me. But I didn't realize that after so many months…you would be…" He sounded so adorably puzzled that Tina laughed. "Am I hurting you?"

Arms wrapped around his shoulders, she looked at him. His hair was damp and sticking to his forehead. His mouth pinched with the control he exercised. Skin pulled taut over his hard features, the depth of his need glimmered in his eyes. "*Si*," she whispered, unable to stem the truth from falling from her lips. She'd forgotten how huge he felt inside her, but it was the panic running amok that she wanted to control. "Give me a moment."

His hands tightened around her hips. "Do you want me to stop?"

"*No!* I… I just need to get used to you again." She wriggled her hips in a small movement. The tightness was still there but something else fluttered beneath it.

A soft kiss against her breastbone. "Take all the time you need."

She hid her face in his shoulder, blinking back the tears that rose. Did they have time? Did he want forever, like she did?

Anchoring her hands on his shoulders, Valentina arched her spine, then moved up and down. The tightness eased. In its wake came little flutters of sensation. She pushed against the sensation, chasing it. Lips pulled first at one nipple and then other, sharpening the little jolts that went to her groin.

Clasping his stubbled jaw, she took his mouth, hard and possessive, letting her kiss speak what she couldn't say. "I want your skin, Kairos. All of you."

In a blink of movement, he brought her to the bed. In the next, he had stripped his shirt, boxers. And then he was prowling on to the bed and she watched him to her heart's content.

The sleek lines of his body. Velvet-rough skin stretched taut over rippling muscles. When he covered her body with his, when he thrust into her, Tina was ready this time.

The drag of their sweat-slicked bodies against each other brought familiar pleasure racing along her nerves. When he thrust, she raised her hips. His grunt of satisfaction made her growl in response.

Hands on her hips, he held her down and yet he was slow, taking his time.

Driving her out of her own skin.

"Faster, please, Kairos. Harder," she urged him on, knowing what he needed. What he desperately craved. Wanting to be everything he needed.

No, not wanting to be.

She *was* everything Kairos needed already. She understood him, she loved him so much, and there wasn't anything she wouldn't face for him. No one she wouldn't fight to be by his side.

All she needed was to make him realize that. To make him understand that she belonged with him.

The realization flew through her veins, turning the moment into so much more than pleasure. He was hers and she would do anything to keep him.

She stroked his broad shoulders, his chest, dug her fingers into his buttocks, tasted the saltiness of his skin. Bit the arch between his neck and shoulders. Possessively, she drank him in.

He pressed a kiss to her temple, his rough thighs grazing her soft ones. "I don't want to hurt you."

"You won't. I can take whatever you give me, Kairos. Don't you know that already?"

As his thrusts became rougher and faster, as his breath hitched, as he growled and his body shuddered on top of her, Tina kissed his temple, breathing the sweat and scent of him.

Whatever his ambitions, whatever had made him into what he was today, she loved all of him. And she would fight for him.

CHAPTER TWELVE

KAIROS COULDN'T HELP HIMSELF. Gathering Valentina to him, he kissed the slope of her shoulder, the skin still damp from their shower an hour ago.

He had pushed her body relentlessly tonight, craving release after release, a need for escape riding him hard. He'd barely soaped her and himself after he'd pushed her against the wall and taken her. Much less toweled them both dry before they had tumbled into bed.

He felt like he had run a triathlon, so sore was his body.

Valentina had, as usual, fallen asleep and nuzzled into him but sleep had evaded him. He'd wanted to leave the bed and her.

Intimacy was always hard on him and the more he'd been determined to limit his increasing need for Valentina to bed, the more she had undone him there.

But last night he hadn't wanted to go. He hadn't

wanted to be alone. No, that wasn't right. He was not going to lie to himself now.

He hadn't wanted to leave *her*. The haven she provided against the cruelty of the world. Against the pain that had filled him.

She was warmth and fire and heaven.

He'd seen her slave hour after hour to make it up to Chiara, to find her place in the fashion world.

He'd seen her care for Theseus and Maria in the last month, responding to their kindness. Worrying about Theseus's health. Persuading a reluctant but smiling Maria into letting her redo her entire wardrobe, because she'd declared impishly to a stunned Theseus that being married to a grouchy bear like him for fifty years, Maria deserved to be dripping in diamonds.

The laughter that had boomed out of Theseus, the shock and gratitude in Maria's eyes that Valentina could make her husband laugh like that again... Theseus had ordered a stunning diamond necklace for Maria on Valentina's advice and when he'd asked Tina to pick something for herself for a present, she'd ask to be counted among his friends, no matter what.

"You like him," he'd said to her later in the privacy of their bedroom. "And he likes you."

"Most people like me, Kairos. I'm fun to be around most of the time. And who wouldn't adore Theseus? Helena is truly poor that she doesn't care for such loving parents. I never knew my father but now I know how to imagine him, at least.

"Theseus...he reminds me of you."

He'd looked at her, shocked. "What?" She couldn't have known what that meant to him.

"Or rather I see what you will be forty years from now. If you..."

He'd backed her against the wall then, something in her expression goading him. "If I what, Valentina?"

"If you learn to be more fun and communicative and a little less brooding."

Before he could punish her for such insolence, she'd slipped away from him.

And in that glimpse of longing and adoration in her eyes when she looked at Theseus, he saw the similarities between them.

Just like him, she had never left that scared, little girl behind. And yet there was fire inside her and for a night, he had wanted what she could give him.

Words never came easily to him and this strange vulnerability she'd created in him robbed him of what little did come.

So, when morning dawned, he had woken her up with kisses and soft caresses, needing to be inside her desperately. Needing to hold her close one more time, needing that intimacy where he could show that he did appreciate her. The only place he could do so.

She had whimpered when he had filled his hands with her breasts.

Arched her behind into him sleepily and whispered, *'Si...'* in that husky tone when he'd hoarsely asked if he could take her like that. So he had slowly stroked himself into her with her back pressed to his chest, her legs caught between his, played with her clit until the need for release was riding her just as hard as it did him. And when her muscles had clenched him even tighter in blissful climax, when she had clung to him, and whispered his name against his own lips again and again, only then did he claim his own release.

And every time his release rushed at him, and he was lost to the pleasure inside her, it felt as if she was stealing some other part of him. As if he was not whole anymore.

But the truth he had learned today, the renewed pain—it was a reminder. He couldn't love Valentina, and he couldn't bear it if…she did the same thing as people who claimed to love him had done.

He would rather hurt her now, keep her whole, than destroy her later, all in the name of love.

When he had woken up this time, she was sitting in the chair he had sat in last night. Freshly showered and dressed in his shirt, she looked the perfect mixture of innocent and siren, a woman capable of tenderness and guts.

Their gazes met and held, the air in the room redolent with the scent of sex and them. Poignant. So much emotion in her eyes that he felt inadequate.

"Come back to bed," he said, pulling the duvet up.

Without a word she crawled back into bed, her trust in him complete.

A faint tension shimmered over her. He kept his arm around her, unwilling to let her retreat from him. Her fingers gripped his forearm, whether asking him to release her or not, he didn't care.

He buried his face in her hair. Tugged her so close that his groin pressed into her buttocks. His chest crushed her back to him. His arm cushioned under her breasts.

"You're not going to ask me about last night?" he whispered.

She pulled his palm to her mouth and pressed a soft kiss. "You will tell me when you're ready."

He stiffened. "What does that mean?"

He felt her exhale, as if she was striving to be patient. "Are you asking to know or to annoy me?"

He swatted her buttocks and she laughed.

Just hearing that sound made his chest lighter.

"It means that whether you share your past or not, whether you continue to act like a gruff bear or a fluffy unicorn, whether you lose your temper or subject me to these heavy silences… nothing changes how I see you, how I think of you. I think, finally—" her voice wobbled and she pressed her face into his hand tightly, before releasing it "—I know the true you, Kairos. Nothing and no one will shake my belief in you. Not even you."

"And if you had seen me in that shower with her?" The question slipped from him, his tone ragged.

"Then I would have dragged her out by her lovely hair and slapped her face. Like I wanted to before you stopped me."

"Your trust in me is that absolute, Valentina?"

"*Si*, it is. Even when I taunted you that you want Theseus's company. I knew the truth, I was just too scared to acknowledge it."

And that implicit trust in her voice broke Kairos down. Words no one had ever heard from him came pouring out. "She told them that I… was the one who got her pregnant."

Valentina jerked, moved in his hold as if to turn around. But he arrested her movement, for he didn't know if he could speak if she pitied him. Slowly, the rigidness in her shoulders eased. A long exhale left her but she gripped his fingers tighter. "Helena?"

"Yes. She… I…one of her high-flying friends, he ran the moment she told him. She and I…we never were close but mostly she tolerated me. Theseus wanted her to show interest in the company and she did, as long as it allowed her extravagant lifestyle. When he learnt that she was pregnant, he became extremely angry. Helena's recklessness never knew bounds but this was too far for him. He threatened to cut her off if she didn't change her ways, if she didn't settle down. She realized that he meant to give me control of everything."

"So she told her parents that you were the one who got her pregnant?"

He could feel her heart racing. Could almost see the conclusions she was running through. He held onto her, long beyond the point where he could fool himself into thinking the comfort was for her.

"Kairos, what did Theseus do?" He felt her kiss his wrist, hold it to her face as if she were bracing herself. For him. Everything she felt—the fear, the worry—it was all for him.

He let it wash over him, let himself bask in it.

"Theseus—" he cleared his throat, wishing for her sake that he was a different man "—decided that Helena and I would marry and possess equal power over the company. He trusted me to keep her in line, I suppose."

"What did you say to his proposal?"

"I agreed. I told him I would do whatever he asked of me."

"You were willing to be a father to some other man's child?"

"Yes. I asked only that he believe that I had never even touched her."

This time, there was no stopping Valentina. She turned in his arms, her gaze peering into his, as if she meant to own everything of him. A bright shine made them glitter. "And he didn't believe you?"

"No. He wouldn't even look at me. I don't think he even cared if Helena and I had been...together. But, however many times I insisted, he wouldn't say that he believed me. By denying his trust... he...he took away everything he had ever given me.

"It felt as if I was that orphan boy again looking through a glass window into what a family looks like." His voice shook. "I don't even remember being angry with Helena's blatant lies. Only crushed by his silence. I...felt betrayed. I told him I didn't want the company if I didn't have his...respect. His trust." His love.

Theseus had chosen Helena's lies over Kairos's truth, and that was what had broken Kairos's heart, why he had left.

Unable to stay still, Tina pulled herself up on

the bed and the sheet with it. Every muscle was tense in his body as if he was living through the ghastly moment again. The anguish in his eyes only showed that she had been right. There was a heart that beat under all that ruthless exterior.

She clasped his jaw and pulled him close. He became still, too rigid, as if he could physically will himself to reject her concern. But she didn't care. All she wanted was to tell him he wasn't alone. That she understood his pain. That it was okay to have loved Theseus so much that it still hurt after all these years.

That he was a good man, one of the best she had ever met. That her brother Leandro, as always, had made the right decision, that he had chosen for her the best man she could ever have asked for.

But she felt too fragile, stretched far too thin after everything they had shared in the last few days.

So she did the only thing she could.

She crawled to him on her knees, the sheet barely covering her breasts and her legs. He watched her with glittering eyes, as if daring her to come closer. Hands on his shoulders, she bent until their noses were touching.

Softly, slowly, she took his mouth. So rigid and hard and yet capable of such tender kisses. Mouth slanted over his, licking the seam of his lips, she willed him to accept it. The sheet slithered down her body, and she heard the hitch in his breath when her nipples grazed his chest.

When he suddenly opened up for her, she plunged her tongue inside. And just like that, the tempo of the kiss changed as he took over.

Even with her body sore in so many places, pleasure inched over her like petals unfurling ever so gently. His fingers wrapped around her neck and he kissed her back hungrily. As if he needed the taste of her to get through this moment. It took but one touch, one stroke, one moment for their hunger to rise, to sweep them away. Their harsh breaths reverberated as he pulled away.

His nostrils flared as he fought for control. He got off the bed, pulled on the shorts he had thrown off some time during the night and looked out the French windows.

She swallowed the words rising through her throat. She would not beg but neither would she retreat. Limbs heavy with exhaustion, she pulled on his discarded shirt and buttoned it down.

Slowly, as if she were dealing with a wounded animal, she reached him and tucked herself into his side until he had to relent. Until he wrapped his hand around her shoulders and pulled her close.

"What happened at the party? Something… changed." It wasn't what Theseus did seven years ago that had cut him.

"I figured out why Theseus didn't believe me seven years ago. Or why he let himself be convinced that Helena was telling the truth."

Breath on a serrated edge, Valentina wrapped her hands around his waist, refusing to be pushed out. Her heart ached for him. His words, his voice reverberated with the depth of his love for Theseus. The rawness of his wound created by Theseus's refusal to trust his word.

"You still came back," she whispered. "You came back when you heard he was sick."

"How could I not? He…" His voice broke and he looked away. "He…gave me the world, Valentina. How could I not rush to his side when he had need of me? When after years of living on the streets, he had shown me compassion, affection? When he made me into everything I am today?"

"You figured out who backed the hostile takeover. That's why you were…" She didn't want him hurt anymore. The notion of him closing down the part of him that cared, it terrified her.

He ran a hand through his hair, his bare chest falling and rising. "Helena was in cahoots with Alexio all along, yes. But it was Maria's stock that tilted the whole thing."

"Maria would have gone against Theseus? But why?" Maria was devoted to her husband. The absolute love and trust between the couple… through everything, they had held together.

Whereas she had avowed love again and again to Kairos, and then run way at the first obstacle.

"I think Theseus wouldn't…didn't believe me over Helena back then because Maria had told him that she'd seen Helena and me…together. In bed."

Tina gasped. "Maria backed Helena's story knowing it was a lie?"

"Helena was desperate and Maria couldn't say no to her daughter. She's always been kind to me and I can almost see how she would think I was getting not a bad deal out of it, that I would be able to control Helena's wildness if we married."

He spoke as if it didn't matter but it was the

clear lack of emotion that told Tina how much it had hurt him to realize what Maria had done.

"You are making excuses for her. And all the guilt, it has been too much for her. That's why she cried on your shoulder like that. That's why she kept saying she was sorry."

Kairos nodded.

"Why give her stock to Helena? Why deceive Theseus?"

"Theseus is stubborn to the core. He…he knew his health was deteriorating, he wouldn't slow down, the company was doing badly. Maria told me that first day she'd been begging him to ask me for help. She'd been terrified about his health. So, coupled with Helena's insistence that it was for the best, I think Maria signed over the proxy on her stock to Helena, which gave Alexio the boost, the vote of confidence to begin turning men loyal to Theseus toward him. Men who were genuinely worried about the company. Men who thought Alexio was the better of two bad choices. Instead, it precipitated Theseus's heart attack."

"But how did you stop it when Maria had already signed it over?" She frowned and then it came to her. "They see you as Theseus's true successor. So when they saw that you had returned, they decided not to back Alexio's coup."

He smiled faintly, but it didn't reach his eyes. "Again, I'm the better choice for the company."

"You can't seriously believe that, Kairos. They treated me like I was part of a family, as if being Kairos Constantinou's wife was something in itself.

"Their trust in you, their confidence is absolute. It is you who always holds himself separate. Who isolates himself. I wish I could make you see it. I wish I could…"

He pulled up their laced fingers and kissed her knuckles. The intimate gesture sent a ray of hope through her. "What?"

"I wish I could change you, just a little."

"Valentina…your trust in me about everything after the way I treated you…it has meant a lot to me. It's a gift I never expected."

"I'm full of surprises like that," she added, trying to lighten the atmosphere. "What happened then?"

"When Maria saw me at Theseus's side within a few hours of his attack, when she saw that all Helena cared about was the company and not her father... I think she started having second thoughts."

"So Helena changed tack, told them that she truly loved you all these years. Since you will not tell Theseus the truth, you had to bring me here. Did you tell him Maria's part in all this? How she deceived him, too?"

Any hesitation she saw in him vanished. His mouth took on that stubborn, uncompromising tilt. "I will not do anything that could harm him. And I forbid you to tell him anything."

"What if Maria will forever continue to assist Helena? Kairos, you didn't see the look in her eyes when he made the announcement. What if, even this evening, Helena had Maria's backing in that...disgusting move?"

White lines fanned around his mouth, and Tina knew that the very real possibility had struck him, too. "It will never be good for both Helena and me to be here. She will only hurt them to get to me, to cut the little trust that there still is between me and Theseus. I can't put Theseus through that. I can't face seeing disillusionment in his eyes again. I will not tell him that his wife of fifty years lied to him to protect their daughter."

"Maria was supposed to protect you, too."

"Listen to me, Valentina. You have to leave what I told you here in this room. I've already started a head hunt for another CEO. An impartial outsider will be good for the company. Helena will be terminated from her position at the company. As soon as I locate her, I will inform her that her stock options will be set up in a trust fund from which she can draw an income, a more than comfortable one. But going forward, she will have no stake in the company. Hopefully that will stop her from trying...to ruin her parents' lives. What she planned two nights ago...it would have broken Theseus. In so many ways." He became again that ruthless man she had lived with for nine months. "I will cut away everything she wants if she doesn't behave."

"And when this is all settled to your satisfaction?"

"I will remain on the board since Theseus insists on signing over his stock to me, and I will oversee things from time to time. Other than that, I'm finished here."

Finished here?

If he could have slammed a door down between them, the message couldn't have been more absolute.

Hands around her waist, Tina swayed against the wall. Even the scent of his skin, the radiating warmth of his body…it felt like they could sear her skin. Tears lumped in her throat, and she breathed deeply, trying to keep them in. "You mean you don't need me anymore in this role," she said almost absently, as if it were happening to someone else.

As if the crack of her heart was outside, not within her.

"*Ne*."

She moved her hand to point behind her toward the once-again rumpled bed. Sometime before or after he had made love to her for the third time, he had carried her to the armchair, pulled the sheets off and made the bed again with clean, crisp bedlinen. When she had looked askance at him, he had winked at her and told her he was nowhere near done.

"What was that then? The four orgasms were parting gifts to remember you by?"

He rubbed a hand over his face. "That was me being selfish, being weak. Needing escape." He looked away and then back, as if he found it hard to focus on her. His features could have been carved in granite for the emotion in them. "Dealing with Maria's lies, Helena's deceit…it has reminded me I have no stomach for this."

"Lie to yourself all you want, Kairos, but don't equate what I feel for you with them."

"Don't make this hard, Valentina. I… I have an upcoming trip to Germany in four days. I'll be gone for almost three weeks. I'm trying to tie up everything before I leave. But even then, I… I think you should return to…"

"To whatever hole I crawled out from?"

He flinched. "Like you pointed out, Helena is going to be furious. She's focused all her anger on me now. I've no idea what she's going to throw at me next and I would rather you were a thousand miles away than here when that happens."

"*Per piacere,* Kairos! Treat me with respect and give me the real reason." Pain crystallized, morphed into fury and Tina embraced it with everything she had. "Shall I send you divorce papers then? Shall I have my powerful brothers throw everything they have at you so that I can take half of everything you own? What does leaving here mean, Kairos? You will damn well spell it out for me!"

When he stayed silent, her heart slipped from her chest.

He simply stared at their clasped hands as if they were talking about the weather. "It will mean divorce. It will mean you can take me for everything I have. You can bring me to my knees."

"You're a bastard!"

"You have no idea how close to the truth you are."

"That's not what I meant. You could have left me well alone. You shouldn't have…you should have let me think you were nothing but a ruthless jerk, Kairos."

He clasped her cheeks with such reverent tenderness that her heart broke a little more. "But I am, Valentina. What I feel for Theseus is gratitude. Don't you see? You were right. It is only a transaction for me. He gave me everything so I repay as much as I can."

"That's not true." She fought against his grip even as he was kicking her out of his life.

"But you… I was wrong about you." Another hard kiss, another piece of her heart forever lost to her. "When Leandro said any intelligent man would know that you are worth more than a hundred companies, he spoke the truth. You deserve everything a man can give you, Valentina. You deserve more than I can give you."

"You're just choosing not to."

"No," Kairos repeated, steeling himself against the bright sheen in her eyes. "I don't know how to love you, Valentina. And I do not wish to learn. Go back to your brothers, *pethi mou*. Tell Leandro, for once in his life, he made a bad bet. Tell him he was wrong about me. Tell him—" Kairos ran his thumb over her lower lip, a cold void opening up inside him "—that I do not deserve the precious gift he gave me."

If only he could embrace it...*this, her.* If only he was capable of giving her what she deserved. Needed.

She felt like home. Like warmth and acceptance. Like a splash of color to his gray canvas. After years of near starving, of no companionship, that was how Maria and Theseus's home had felt. He had been so cautious at first, but eventually they had won him over. He hadn't asked for anything but they had given kindness, care and love again and again, in so many ways.

Until he had believed it all. Until he had forgotten the cautiousness he had learned on the streets. Until he had forgotten the wretchedness of being alone.

Until he had started loving them, until they had simply become a part of him.

And then everything had been taken away. In one moment, everything had been lost. Seven years ago and now again…

If he trusted Valentina, if he opened himself up to everything she made him feel and things fell apart…it would be so much worse. A million times more painful. And he would break this time. If she took it away like Theseus and Maria had done, if suddenly he found himself all alone after having had a taste of…

Oxhi!

That was a fate he couldn't even indulge in.

He was not ready for the weight of her love.

He was never going to be ready for her.

For this.

For them.

She would only starve for affection with him. He'd already trampled her spirit. If he broke her because he couldn't love her, he couldn't bear it.

"You're right." She pushed the silky mass of her hair away angrily, the innate sensuality of the gesture stealing his breath. "You don't deserve me. I always thought I was not good enough for you. That I had to earn your love somehow. But this has nothing to do with me. *You're* the coward, Kairos. You're unworthy of me, not the other way around. You want to choose a miserable existence instead of trusting me, instead of taking a chance on us, fine. Then please stay in the other bedroom until you leave for your trip."

Her words hit him hard. "I can have you flown back to Milan tonight."

She backed out of his reach, a fiery tenacity to her expression. His shirt hung on her, baring most of her sleek thighs. Curves he'd never touch or feel wrapped around himself again. "I'm not leaving, you are."

He jerked his gaze back up, the void in his gut only deepening. "Valentina—"

"I have three more weeks left with Chiara. People are counting on me to do my job. I will not let them down, I will not let myself down because you've decided you've had enough of playing marriage. I will not disappear in the middle of the night from Theseus and Maria's lives as if I had done something wrong. As if I'm responsible for this debacle."

"I don't want you here," Kairos said before he could stop himself. Her mouth pinched into a thin line. "Helena—"

"I can handle Helena. At the least, I know what to expect from her. I want to finish my work here, work the contacts I made. Maria will need someone to look after her, too." She gazed at him for a few seconds that felt like an eternity. He couldn't bear the disillusionment in her eyes. Broken hope.

He took a step toward her, but she shook her head and backed away. "Goodbye, Kairos."

CHAPTER THIRTEEN

KAIROS STARED AT the society pages of a leading online fashion magazine, his breath hurtling through his chest and throat like a hurricane.

Valentina was laughing in this picture, standing in between her friend Nikolai and Ethan King—an American textile magnate whose burgeoning alliance with Conti Luxury Goods was all the rage in the news.

He'd known Leandro had been hunting for a new CEO for the board of CLG for months now. The initial prize he had promised Kairos himself. The prize Kairos had thought important enough to take Valentina on.

Thee mou, he'd been such an arrogant fool.

Leandro had stepped down himself after he had discovered he had a child with Alexis seven years ago. When Kairos had looked askance, he'd laughed and said that he would understand one day.

Luca had married Sophia, who headed her

stepfather's company Rossi's. The playboy genius still did his own thing, as he had always done. He'd never had any interest in CLG except to thwart Kairos because Luca had assumed that Kairos would only hurt their sister. He'd been right.

Ethan King was a good choice. For the CLG board.

His gaze returned to her in the picture.

She'd fashioned her silky hair to fall over one side. A pink pantsuit made everything of her long legs. A thin chain glittered at her neck and disappeared into the neckline of her blouse.

Frantically, he clicked through more pictures to see if she'd kept the pendant he had bought for her. But he couldn't spot it.

Christos! What was he doing?

Her arms around Nikolai and Ethan, her eyes glittering with laughter, she looked gorgeous.

She looked…*happy.*

Seven weeks since he'd last seen her. Since she'd told him defiantly that she'd finish her position before she left. Since he'd walked out of her life for good.

By the time he had returned from Germany,

she'd been gone. Every trace of her removed from their bedroom, from the villa.

The first time she had left he'd been so angry.

This time, it felt like she had taken a part of him with her. As if she'd ripped him apart, never to be whole. Everything was so blank, so dull since he'd returned. As if all the color in the world had been leached out.

He'd been so sure that he'd done the right thing by her. For once, he'd put her happiness, her well-being before his. Before his own ambitions.

Somehow, he'd been getting through his days.

Until she'd sent him divorce papers.

Until suddenly, she'd exploded into the news again in true Valentina fashion. She'd partnered with Sophia to launch a full-service fashion boutique—for clients who had personal styling needs and a host of other services.

She had collaborated with major fashion brands to launch an online vlog in which she had models of different sizes showcase the latest creations from designer brands.

The camera loved Valentina. She was a natural.

The vlog had exploded within a week of launching, drawing more than a million hits on the internet and her business had taken off.

She'd already hosted a fashion show on a morning talk show to advertise her services. Stylish and sophisticated, she was already adored by the media. She had appeared in numerous TV style segments.

His heart in his throat, he clicked Play on a small news clip that had been recorded on another talk show.

"I always used to think my talent was useless. But then I learned that I was wasting my potential by denying myself the connections I did have. So I partnered with my sister-in-law and launched the boutique. It was she who gave me the idea. Sophia, for example, is an exceptional businesswoman but had always had problems dressing herself because she—" a fond laugh here "—she wasn't as she says, 'a giraffe with legs that go on forever.' She's curvy and sexy, and it was my pleasure to help her find clothes that showcased her body, to make her feel confident in her own shape.

"I love dressing people and now I can put my expertise into making someone else feel comfortable in their own skin. Be confident in themselves while they go out to capture the world. Everyone needs fashion advice..." She hesitated and then laughed—that husky full-bodied sound—when her brothers walked onto the stage in matching dark gray suits. She stood up and walked to them until they were both standing on her sides. "Even my handsome, powerful brothers, the legendary Conti men."

Kairos closed his laptop hard. He had watched the same damn clip a hundred times.

Leandro and Luca had walked onto the show to give their support to their sister—a spectacular publicity move he was sure had been orchestrated by Sophia, to thrust Valentina's fashion venture into the limelight. With their backing, with Sophia's business acumen and Valentina's own talent, he had no doubt her business would reach unprecedented heights.

She had found her place in the world.

He should be happy that she had taken his advice. That she had used what was at her disposal to fuel her dream, to launch her dream career.

He should be happy that he hadn't…damaged her permanently.

But then Valentina had an unquenchable spirit, a fierce strength, a generous heart. She drew people to her wherever she went.

If not today, if not this month, if not this year,

she would find that happily-ever-after that she so desperately wanted. Some man would see what a beautiful person she was, inside and out, and love her as she deserved.

Suddenly the picture of Ethan King and her laughing into the camera at some new nightclub he was launching flashed in his mind's eye.

With a curse, he strolled to the bay windows.

Would Leandro go down that path again? Would Valentina let him find her a husband again? Or had she already found someone who did appreciate what an extraordinary woman she had grown into?

Had she finished with him already?

Bile rose through his throat at the thought of the man holding his wife, touching her, kissing her. At the thought of Valentina surrendering all that passion, surrendering her heart to another man.

A breeze ruffled the papers he had left on the side table. He should just sign the divorce papers and be done with her.

Give her whatever she wanted.

Release her from this marriage. Release himself from the grip she seemed to have on his heart. Be done with it.

He'd made the safe choice, for once in his life,

so why couldn't he just live with it? Why couldn't he accept it and move on?

"Kairos?"

He turned around to see Maria standing at the door, wary and hesitant.

He frowned, wondering how long she'd been standing there. He'd mostly avoided her since the night of their anniversary party and she had let him.

"Does Theseus need something?"

"*Oxhi.* He's resting." She looked at her hands and then back up again. "I… I wish to speak to you. Do you have a few minutes for me?"

"Of course," he said, forcing himself to move from his spot.

He watched her silently as she flitted around the room restlessly. As always, she was elegantly dressed in a dark sweater and neatly pressed white capri pants. Her nails had been done with that signature red color for as long as he could remember. Her hair had grayed considerably, still cut into a short bob.

Only now did he realize how much weight she had lost in the last year. She'd been tirelessly caring for Theseus for so many months now. Not to mention whatever hell Helena had put her through.

He poured out water from a jug and placed a glass for her on the side table.

"Is everything okay?" he prompted, her restlessness increasing his own anxiety.

"No. It is not."

"What can I do to help?"

"You would help, Kairos, still?"

Something in her gaze made him uncomfortable. "Of course, I would, Maria. You have but to command me."

A brittle laugh fell from her mouth. "Theseus is right. I am a foolish woman."

He hardened himself against the emotion twisting his gut. It had to be about Helena, about all the decisions he'd been making about the company.

He could take whatever she threw at him, he reminded himself. He could take it and still stay standing. After all, Helena was her daughter and he was…an outsider.

Since the minute Theseus had decided he would adopt Kairos, Maria had welcomed him unflinchingly. She had only ever shown him kindness. And he would pay it back a million times over.

"Maria, whatever it is, you can say it to me without hesitation. I understand how hard this must be for you. And whatever you request for Helena, I promise I will try to do my best to accommodate it. I just can't… I can't let her be a part of the company anymore. Not if I have to do what's best for the business. And for Theseus and you."

She flicked another wary glance at his face and then away. Then she sat down and gestured for him to do the same. Her head down, she looked at her clasped fingers. When she looked up, there were tears in her eyes.

Tears that cut through his heart.

"He's so angry with me. So angry. But it was the right thing to do," she half muttered to herself.

Any walls he had erected against her crumbled at the sight of her tears. He took her hands in his. "Maria, what are you talking about?"

"Can you believe it…in fifty years of marriage, today is the first time he wouldn't look at me. The first time he said he was disappointed in me. He is ashamed of me, and I deserve it."

He sat back, shocked. "You and Theseus never fight."

"I told him everything. Everything Helena ever did. Everything I shielded from him. Everything she…lied about. About the pregnancy. About the stock and the takeover. About…my part in it. About all the disgusting things she'd planned to do to discredit you in his eyes."

"What?" Shock robbed his words. "Is…is Theseus okay? *Thee mou,* Maria! What would that accomplish except jeopardize his health? The last thing he needs just when he is finally recuperating is to learn that you—"

"That I betrayed him. That I betrayed everything he has always stood for." All the hesitation was gone from her face. "That I treated you so horribly."

"You didn't. You…only ever showed me kindness." He walked away, unable to look into her eyes. Unable to stop the dam within him from bursting. "Theseus brought me home, yes, but you welcomed me with open arms. You encouraged me when I thought I would never leave behind my dirty roots. You…gave me everything, Maria. More than I had a right to."

"But I didn't love you like I should love a son. When he told me that day that he wanted to raise you, that he had decided it, in true arrogant Theseus fashion—" laughter burst through the tears running down her cheeks "—that you were our son now, I promised him I would love you like one. That I would embrace you in every way. But I did not. I…was weak. I let my love for Helena blind me. She came so late into our lives…when I had given up on the idea of a child completely that I didn't see how much I was spoiling her."

"You don't need to explain."

"I do. I need to. I didn't just let Theseus down, and you down. I let myself down, too."

He felt her stand next to him, the subtle floral perfume she always wore twisting through him. His belly clenched, the scent of her enveloping him in kindness, filling him with longing. Filling him with an endless need for acceptance, for love.

His jaw clenched, a lump of emotion in his throat. "She is your daughter. I do not begrudge you your love for her. I never expected to be the same. Believe me, I understand. I…never expected more." But he hadn't been able to stop himself from wanting it anyway. From needing it.

"Oh, but it is your right to have everything, Kairos. It is your right to be loved unconditionally, not to be second to her. It is what I promised myself that day we brought you home with us. I'm sorry for forgetting that. You're everything Theseus said you would be. You are not just his. You're *my* son, too, and I am so sorry for…my actions."

"Please—"

"Will you forgive me, Kairos? Will you forgive my foolish hope in thinking that she would change, for thinking she deserved one more chance every time? Will you forgive me for not loving you as I should have?"

She was openly sobbing now, and the sight of it broke his heart.

Kairos took her in his arms and she came with a soft cry. Tears pooled in his own eyes and he held them back by sheer will. "Shh… Maria. I cannot bear to see you like this. I forgive you. Of course, I forgive you." His words rushed out of him, a jagged crack in his heart healing over.

A lightness he had never known filled his chest. "I… I've been fortunate enough to have two mothers, Maria. I never realized how fortunate I was. I… Please, calm yourself. I can't bear to see you cry. I did everything to shield you and Theseus from her. I… She's left me no other way to stop her. I never wanted anything that should have been hers. All I wanted was to make you and Theseus proud of me. All I wanted was…" He forced himself to speak the words he'd always denied himself. To acknowledge the need inside. To admit that loving Theseus and Maria had only made him stronger, not weaker, as he had always believed. "…your love."

She wiped her tears and looked at up at him with sad eyes.

"I know, Kairos. I know you did more than a flesh-and-blood brother would have done for her. I know all the allowances you made for Helena. I know that, despite all the stupid games she played with you, you've never spoken a word against her to Theseus. You took your cue from me. You gave me even more loyalty and love than you gave Theseus. I didn't realize that until he pointed out. Until he said we did have a child who loved us more than anything in the world. You don't owe her anymore.

"There's a certain freedom in letting go, isn't there? She came to see me yesterday, you know. I told her in no uncertain terms that I would be part of her crazy schemes no more. Theseus told me about the trust fund idea you set up and you've been more generous than even he would have been. So let us hope this time she will truly change, *ne*?"

Kairos simply nodded, unable to form words. Unable to staunch the love that flowed within his veins. His world already felt different, lighter, brighter. He felt as if he were a new man, as if everything was possible now.

As if he could let himself—

"What is this?" Maria said, taking the sheaf of documents he had left on the table. "Divorce proceedings? You and Valentina are separating?" Shock punctured very word. "I thought she left because she missed her brothers. She promised Theseus she would see him for Christmas. She…"

He had no idea what she'd seen in his eyes before he looked away. "She left me even before I came back here, before Theseus's heart attack."

"You said it had just been a small misunderstanding. Why did you bring her here then? Oh… to tell us that you were already taken." Her hand on his shoulder turned him. "Did she want to leave again when you'd accomplished everything?"

"No." Even then, she had willed him to understand. Even then, she had given him another chance. Then another chance. What a heartless man he was to have turned her away! What a coward! "I sent her away."

"And she went away dutifully? For some reason, that doesn't suit her. Why did you send her away?"

"It was for her own good. I... Valentina...she's like a storm that ravages everything in its path, in a good way. I... I have nothing to give her, Maria. She deserves better than a man like me."

Something sad flitted in Maria's eyes. She took his hands in hers, and the simple touch calmed the furor in his gut. But nothing could ever fill the void his wife had left in his life. In his heart.

"A more honorable, kinder man, Kairos? A man who could love her more than you already do? A man who needs her so desperately that he walks around like an empty shell?"

Something jerked in the deep crevices of his being. His denial froze on his lips. He could not lie. Not to her, and not to himself.

For he did love Valentina. With every breath in him. With every cell in his body.

He had fallen for her long before he had even understood what it meant.

"I rejected her one too many times. I starved her when all she'd needed was a kind word. I hurt her again and again until whatever she might have felt for me died. I don't know how to love her, Maria. I don't know if I can give her what she needs. I don't know if I could bear it if she… if she stopped loving me. She would destroy me then."

Maria enfolded her arms around him. It was a mother's embrace, something he had longed for for so long, something he had needed for so long. The fear and anguish he had been fighting for weeks flooded him.

"Oh… Kairos. Trust yourself, trust the bond between you two. And trust her love for you."

He nodded, hope unfurling within him. His wife had a generous heart. He had to trust his into her keeping. He had to take the biggest risk of his life if he wanted her.

And he did want her.

Pulling back from the hug, Maria laughed. "How about you and I make a pact? We shall be brave and beg for forgiveness from the ones we love, *ne*?"

He laughed at her suggestion, sobered at the wary glance she cast toward Theseus's bedroom. He kissed her cheek, breathing in her scent one more time. Willing her to lend him a fraction of the courage she had.

"We will be brave in love, together," he whispered.

She nodded, kissed both his cheeks. "You will not stay away for another seven years, will you, Kairos?"

"No, I won't. This is not goodbye, Maria. Valentina and I will spend Christmas here."

She nodded and hugged him again, and in her embrace, Kairos found the strength he needed.

The strength to love the woman who had stolen his heart a long time ago.

CHAPTER FOURTEEN

THE LAST THING Kairos wanted to face, when all he wanted was to see and touch Valentina, was a battalion of overbearing, interfering, annoying Contis.

Yet when he had finally bulldozed his way into Villa De Conti on the banks of Lake Como almost three weeks later, on a crisp November evening, the family, including the patriarch Antonio, were assembled around the ornate dining table, all staring up at him, mostly with varying degrees of anger, mistrust and doubt.

Except Leandro's little girl Isabella, who instantly wrapped her arms around him for a quick hug.

"Hello, Isabella," he said returning her hug.

Sophia stared at him with searching eyes. Whatever she had seen there, she pushed her chair back and embraced him.

"I'm not going to ask you how you are," she whispered, only for his ears. "You look awful."

"You know what she's capable of," he answered in kind, not even pretending to misunderstand.

"You deserved it."

Suddenly, panic-fueled urgency filled him. "Do I have a chance, Sophia?"

She betrayed nothing. "That's for her to tell you, Kairos." She smiled fondly then. "Always calculating the odds before you take the leap, *si*? It will not work in this."

He could never understand how smart, sensible Sophia could tolerate the charming scoundrel that was the Conti Devil, but then he still didn't understand what his vivacious wife had ever seen in him to love.

"Being married suits you," he said with a smile.

She blushed before going back to her place next to her husband.

"What the hell do you want now?" Luca growled at him from the top end of the table, sitting exactly opposite Leandro on the other side.

"I wish to speak to my wife."

"She's not here."

"You're lying. And I will beat you to a bloody pulp and mar that pretty face if you get in my way again."

Utter silence descended over the table.

"Don't you think you've hurt her enough?" Again from the crazy genius. "Not counting the fact that you endangered her by letting loose that woman on Tina."

Kairos didn't know what he was doing until he had Luca's shirt bunched in his shoulders. The fear inside him knew no bounds. "What the hell are you talking about?"

Something in his tone must have communicated itself to him, because Luca's voice softened. "Helena came to see Valentina at work and caused a huge scene. I was there thankfully, and I think Tina talked some sense into her."

"Also, Tia Tina told me she slapped that horrible woman," Izzie piped up. "Oops, I wasn't supposed to tell you guys that."

Thee mou, what had Helena done to hurt Valentina?

Luca loosened his shirt from Kairos's grip. "I honestly don't think you're right for her. All you have caused her so far is pain."

The barb stuck home but Kairos forced himself to ignore Luca. Instead he addressed Leandro, who had always been the more sensible one.

"I have been trying for three weeks to see her. To contact her. She's still my damned wife. I should have been told Helena was here. It is I who brought Valentina into her focus. I should have been—" He couldn't even get the words out.

"Tina forbade us, Kairos," Sophia added softly.

"You've no right to stop me. To block my attempts." The stunt that Luca had pulled a week ago when he had ferried Valentina away on his beastly bike while Kairos had been waiting in the front lounge made his blood boil.

Leandro sighed. "She doesn't want to see you. And I will not lose her by interfering again, just when she is back in our lives."

"I'm not asking for your interference. I'm asking you to stay out of this. She is mine—to protect and to hold on to." The ragged words escaped before he could stop them.

Every gaze looked upon him with varying degrees of shock and pity now.

Leandro's wife, Alexis, shrugged. "He has a point, Leandro. You're still protecting her."

"Have you seen the look she gets in her eyes when she thinks no one's looking at her?" Luca demanded of Alexis.

"*Si*, Luca. We have all seen it," Sophia responded, with a hand over his shoulder. "And that tells me more than anything that we should give Kairos a chance. We all make mistakes."

"Not the same one, twice," Luca added meaningfully.

"She's in the garden," Alexis added hurriedly. "And she has a guest, so maybe you should wait."

"Who?"

"Ethan King," Luca said with a wicked smile, twisting the knife a little in Kairos's gut.

Sophia sent him a warning glance. "He's been talking to her about investment opportunities in her new boutique."

Kairos had heard enough. With a muttered curse, he made his way to the garden when Izzie pointed out, "They're not in the garden anymore. I saw them going up the stairs, into her bedroom."

Valentina had barely settled in the sitting room of her suite and pulled up her website analytics with Ethan when her hand hit the glass of white wine she had poured for him.

Cursing to herself, she mopped up the wine from the sofa and was about to hand him the napkin when the door of her bedroom opened with a hard slam. It hit the wall, then swung forward until Kairos stopped its momentum.

His gaze took in her outstretched hand over Mr. King's shirt and thunder dawned in the silver gaze.

Before she could think, she guiltily snatched her hand back. And then regretted the move.

He had no rights over her. She had done nothing to be guilty about, either.

He stared at her with such naked emotion shining in his eyes that it took her a few minutes to process the surge of her own feelings. And then pathetically, once again, she landed on hope in the end.

Her heart pounded with that same eagerness that she had tried to curb since the moment she had realized he was back in Milan. That he had been trying to see her.

But she was so tired of that hope. Exhausted from the weight of it.

"I would like to speak with you," he said, almost successful in packing away all the emotion radiating from him. "In private. At length."

"I'm not free right now," she offered softly. "Ethan only has this one hour before he leaves for the States. I've been waiting for weeks for a chance to speak with him."

His gaze flew to her open laptop and then back to her. Uncertainty and hesitation and something else flickered in his gaze. He had never looked so vulnerable.

"Take as long as you need. I will wait outside," he said and her heart slipped a little.

Over the next few minutes, she tried to corral her thoughts. But the business proposal she had put together with Sophia's help blurred. The statistics she meant to show Ethan zigzagged, her heart focused on the man waiting outside the door for her.

He had never waited for her. He had never looked at her as if his heart was in his eyes.

Sick of the turmoil in her gut, she finally apologized to Ethan and the gentleman that he was, he was nice about it and excused himself from the room.

The door had barely closed behind him when Kairos reached her.

A white shirt and black trousers hugged his powerful physique. Dark shadows circled his eyes and instead of the satisfaction she wanted to feel, all she suffered was a soft ache.

He looked so tired. She knew how hard he worked. But more than that, she knew what a toll it would have taken on him to finish what he had started with Helena and the company.

She ached to hold him, to love him, to offer him the comfort he desperately needed. But he wouldn't allow it. He needed her but he would never admit it.

"Why is it that I always have to chase you—" his nostrils flared "—and then find you with a man in some intimate situation?"

"Maybe the question you should be asking is why is it that you're always chasing me," she countered. "What is it that you do that makes me run from you in the first place?"

He flinched and she wrapped her arms around herself. She had promised herself she wouldn't do this. She wouldn't beg. She wouldn't complain. She would want nothing from him.

But seeing him after so many weeks, she could barely breathe, barely keep herself together.

How had she forgotten how he dwarfed everything with his presence? How he took over her very breath when he was near?

"I saw the clip from the talk show. And the vlog…that was a stroke of genius."

"*Si?*"

"I knew you had it in you. I'm glad for your success, Valentina."

"I owe it to you," she said softly.

"That internship with Chiara—"

"No, it was your criticism that I was doing nothing with my life that egged me on. I wanted to prove you wrong. To show you that I could be successful, too. Only I realized how much I enjoy it. That I'm good at it. You did teach me that I could be more than the shallow, vapid Valentina, more than what the Conti genes amount to. But you also made me realize that my value as a person doesn't depend on whether I'm a success or a failure. That I'm my own person and it is your loss if you can't love me."

How many times could one's heart break?

When she tried to step back, he clasped her arm to stop her. "Don't—" he cleared his throat "—do not retreat from me, Valentina."

Her heart crawled into her throat at the rough need he couldn't hide in his voice. "Why are you here, Kairos?"

"First, please tell me Helena didn't hurt you."

"Is that why you're here? To make sure she

didn't do me lasting damage? Out of guilt?" She couldn't keep the disappointment out of her voice.

"No, I didn't know until Luca told me a few minutes ago. I'm sorry, Valentina. I should have realized—"

"She didn't hurt me, Kairos. I was actually recording the vlog when she stormed into the studio at Conti Towers. I don't think even she realized how far gone she was. She ranted that you were cutting her off, that she would make you pay for it. And that she knew how to make you suffer. I couldn't take it. I slapped her so hard that my arm still hurts. It was dramatic, almost soap-opera-like, but sometimes that's what it takes, *si*?

"I told her I would tell Theseus everything she had ever done if she didn't quietly accept what you were giving her. And then she would truly be on the streets. I told her I would set my powerful brothers loose on her if she ever came near you again. If she ever hurt you again. And I think it was helpful that Luca looked exceptionally scruffy and dangerous that day—he'd been on one of his days-without-sleep composing binge, and I think for once my threats got through—"

"I love you."

"Got through to her and she…she…" Words

stuck in her throat, lodged beneath her heart. Had she imagined the words? Had she… "What did you say?"

"*S'agapao*, Valentina. So much that it terrifies me. So much that I can't sleep or eat or drink."

He fell to his knees in front of her, and Tina thought she might be hallucinating. She was afraid that she was only imagining this, that it was another dream haunting her sleep…no words came.

Until he wrapped his arms around her and buried his face in her belly. So tight that she could barely breathe.

The scent of him hit her like a thunderstorm, sinking into her pores.

He was real, this was real. The arms holding her…the soft kisses he was planting on her belly, the huffs of his breath feathering over her skin, it was all real.

He looked up then and the love shining in his eyes stole her breath all over again. "I'm crazy about you. I love your teasing smiles, your penchant for drama, your unswerving loyalty, your generous heart." His palm rested on her chest. The thud of her heart was loud enough to roar through the room. "I love your long legs, your small breasts, your perfect skin, but more than anything I love you, *agapi mou*. I love how you love me. I love that you fight so bravely for the ones you love. I love that you make me a better man, that you fill my life with so much color and drama and noise—"

She laughed at that and he laughed and then she was in his arms. Kissing him hungrily amidst sobbing. He tasted of love and acceptance and home. Palms clasping his jaw, she kissed him until she couldn't breathe anymore. But the tears refused to stop.

She knew how much he hated tears so she buried her face in his neck. The scent of him, the taste of his skin finally calmed her.

"Shh, *moru mou*. No more tears. I would rather cut out my heart then be apart from you ever again. I was a fool not to understand how much you love me. How much I already loved you. A coward to believe that you would take it away on a whim.

"I was so afraid of hurt that I didn't even realize how long I have loved you.

"I think it started the first time even. You wore an emerald green dress that bared your entire back and you had been standing amidst your admirers and when Leandro called for you, there had been such unconditional love in your eyes, such open affection... I think I was struck immediately." His words made her gasp and she fought for her breath.

They didn't come easily to him, she knew. And she loved him all the more for it.

His palm stroked up and down her back tenderly, a torrent of endearments rushing out of him amidst a million apologies.

She felt his kiss at her temple, his shallow breaths as if, just like her, he was still unsure that she was here in his arms. "Valentina?"

"*Si?*"

"I should like to hear you say it, *pethi mou*. I am dying inside with the fear that I might have pushed you away one too many times, that finally you have realized that—"

She placed her finger on his lips.

"I love you, Kairos. I always will. I love you, knowing that you are stubborn, and ruthless and reserved. But I also love you knowing that you're kind, wonderful and extremely generous when it comes to orgasms. I recently read in some magazine that very few men actually go down on a woman whereas they expect the return all the time?"

Only his wife could insert the statistics about blow jobs into the conversation while he was pouring his heart out.

Kairos laughed, picked her up and followed her down to her bed.

He tugged her to him and kissed her some more. A lot more. Hard, consuming kisses. Soft, needy kisses. Tongues and teeth, they clung to each other until the need for air forced them apart.

He stripped her clothes and his with an urgency that devoured him.

And then she was naked for him. Long, sleek limbs toned with muscle. Small pouty breasts with lush nipples. She was perfect and she was his.

She reached out her hand to him, no shadows in her eyes. Nothing but abiding love and sultry temptation. "Come to me, please. I have missed you."

"Not more than I missed you." He growled against her mouth. "I can't be slow, *pethi mou*. Not today. I… I don't want to hurt you."

"You won't, Kairos. Trust me. Trust this thing between us, *si*?"

"Si." But there was nothing he could do to stem his urgent need.

He kissed her breasts, her belly, her legs, every inch of her perfect skin. When she scratched his back, just as frantic as him, he pushed his fingers into her wet heat. As deep as she could take him.

The need riding her, her body arching off the bed when he massaged her clit, the sheen of her skin...that calmed his need.

The scent of her arousal, that she had always wanted him, that she had again chosen him to love...it calmed the furor in his blood.

He sucked on her nipples, relentlessly pushing her to the edge until she fractured around his fingers. Until tremors built and ebbed in her slender body.

And then when the edge of their hunger for each other had been taken off, when she had calmed enough to believe that he wasn't going anywhere, he sat up, pulled her into his embrace until she was straddling him and then he thrust into her snug heat.

Arms around his back, mouths glued to each other's, they made slow, lazy love. All he wanted was to be inside her. To be surrounded by her warmth. To love her for as long as there was breath in his body.

"I love you, Valentina," he whispered, before he increased his thrusts, before release claimed his soul.

Hours later, Kairos emerged from deep sleep. His hand shot out instantly searching for his wife.

When he found her, his heartbeat returned to normal.

After he had toppled them both off the edge and into exhaustion for the third time, she had snuck down to the kitchen and had assured her family that he hadn't killed her, for she had heard them outside the door, muttering and arguing,

They had devoured the cheese and fruit plate she had brought upstairs. The white wine—he had lapped it off her breasts, her tummy and her soft folds. Whatever he did, however many times release clashed through him, it wasn't enough.

He pulled her down to lie alongside him. Her back to his chest, she cozily nuzzled into him. "I'm never going to get enough of you, I'm never going to let you go," he said, unable to cover the fierceness of his tone.

"Nor will I you," she said in a low, sleep-mussed voice. "We will have a big family, maybe four, five kids...boisterous, dramatic, noisy kids like me and we will drive you up the wall."

"That sounds like paradise."

"Kairos?"

The uncertainty still in her voice gutted him. "Yes?"

"Are you still looking for a job?"

He laughed and turned her over until she was facing him. Propping himself up on an elbow, he placed a lazy kiss on her mouth. "I am. I have offers from a few MNCs to do some house cleaning but nothing I'm interested in. We can live wherever you want. Do whatever we want. I'm not in a particular hurry to return to work."

"No. I know you're busy and that's fine but I just want to spend time with you. Have those four or five kids after a couple of years maybe?"

"*Si.* I...told Maria that we would spend Christmas with them." He frowned. "I'm sorry. I should have realized that you might want to spend it with your family."

"How about New Year with the Contis instead?"

This time, she rose up and claimed him for a soft kiss. "Hopefully by then Luca and I will be able to tolerate being in the same room."

She laughed, and then sobered. "You and Maria talked?"

"She told Theseus everything."

Her tight hug said so many things words could not. He let himself bask in the warmth of it. A hundred years together and he wouldn't have enough of Valentina.

She combed her fingers through his hair and sighed. "I have a proposal for you. But you don't have to accept it."

"Sounds important," he said trying to sound encouraging.

"I would like to live in Milan for a bit, with the boutique taking off it seems like a perfect fit."

"Valentina, we can live wherever you want, as long as we're together."

"Leandro is still looking for a CEO. He's—"

"Oxhi!"

"Kairos, please listen to me. He told me you've always been the perfect candidate. He trusts you. And I think…as the Conti heiress's loving husband, it is your right."

"I never wanted to do anything that would make you doubt my love for you."

"You won't. This doesn't. *Ti amo*, Kairos, and

no job you take, no woman who wants you, will change that."

Joy suffusing his very soul, Kairos said yes to his wife.

And he meant to say yes for a very long time— to everything she asked.

* * * * *

LET'S TALK

Romance

For exclusive extracts, competitions
and special offers, find us online:

- **f** facebook.com/millsandboon
- 📷 @millsandboonuk
- 🐦 @millsandboon

Or get in touch on 0844 844 1351*

For all the latest titles coming soon,
visit millsandboon.co.uk/nextmonth

*Calls cost 7p per minute plus your phone company's price per
minute access charge